A Year
in Story
& Song

An Hachette UK Company
www.hachette.co.uk

The authorized representative in the EEA is Hachette Ireland,
8 Castlecourt Centre, Dublin 15, D15 XTP3, Ireland (email: info@hbgi.ie)

First published in Great Britain in 2024 by Gaia, an imprint of
Octopus Publishing Group Ltd
Carmelite House
50 Victoria Embankment
London EC4Y 0DZ
www.octopusbooks.co.uk

This material was previously published in *The Almanac: A Seasonal
Guide to 2019*, *The Almanac: A Seasonal Guide to 2020*, *The Almanac: A
Seasonal Guide to 2021* and *The Almanac: A Seasonal Guide to 2022*.

ISBN 978-1-8567-5548-1

A CIP catalogue record for this book is available from the British Library.

Printed and bound in the United Kingdom.

10 9 8 7 6 5 4 3

Publishing Director: Stephanie Jackson
Publisher: Lucy Pessell
Designer: Isobel Platt
Assistant Editor: Samina Rahman
Production Manager: Caroline Alberti
Cover illustration: Gemma Trickey

MIX
Paper | Supporting
responsible forestry
FSC® C104740

A Year in Story & Song

A celebration of the seasons

From the bestselling author of
THE
ALMANAC

LIA LEENDERTZ

Contents

A Year in Story and Song

We humans love stories. We love to hear them and to tell them, around fires and by bedsides, and we love to use them to make sense of the world around us. The seasons, in all their ever-changing variety, give us many opportunities for storytelling. I have been making *The Almanac*, my seasonal guide to each year, since 2018, and every year within it I have sought out and told some of the year's stories and songs. Many are brought together here.

The year and its seasons tell a story. It begins dark and chilled, but soon bursts open into the life and zest and sunshine of spring. Summer brings a flowering of romance, warm breezes and lengthy twilights, and then autumn – a time of plenty, of ripening and harvesting and bringing in. Finally, the year retreats again, and settles down into a time of dreaming and dark.

I have dug out those stories and songs that mark and celebrate the activities and festivities of each season: the full moons and their names, Epiphany in January, St Patrick's Day in March, May Day, Midsummer, Hallowe'en and more. They feature mischievous boggarts and fairies, saints and sailors, leprechauns and dragons, pilgrimages and charms, milk maids and rose queens, Robin Hood and the Green Man. The songs range from shanties and love songs, to bawdy ballads and wassails, to carols and rounds, and have been sung for hundreds of years, often at particular moments in the calendar. With this book you can now bless your apple trees with a wassail in January and serenade your love with a carol on Midsummer's Eve, joining a thread of voices stretching back through time.

For me, this process of telling, reading, singing and listening to the stories and songs of the year provides a vibrant echo of past lives and past ways of celebrating and marking the turning of the year: they are pieces of history that feel alive and spirited, and that we can be a part of. I hope you are tempted to include these stories and songs in your traditions too, and that they add a little magic to your own journey through each year.

January

The Naming of January

Faoilleach (Scots Gaelic)
Januar (Scots/Ulster Scots) | *Eanáir* (Irish Gaelic)
Jerry-gueree (Manx) | *Ionawr* (Welsh)
Genver (Cornish) | *Janvyi* (Jèrriais)
Iveskero (Romani)

The word Faoilleach in Scots Gaelic originally referred to a period of winter, but has come to mean specifically January in modern Scots Gaelic. It comes from *faol-chu* which means 'wolf', and this gives a glimpse into Scotland's wilder past Januarys, as there have been no wolves in Scotland for hundreds of years (the last wolf having been slain by legendary deerstalker MacQueen of Findhorn in 1743). Wolves' howling reaches its height in January in mating season as the males compete for mates, before falling quiet during the denning season.

All of the other words for January from the various languages of the British Isles appear to be variants on the Latin *Januarius*. This may have arisen from either the Latin for 'door', *ianua* (the door onto the year), or the Roman god Janus, the god of transitions and beginnings, traditionally depicted as having two faces, one looking back into the past and one looking ahead to the future.

Romani Names for the Months

Since the 16th century, following their migration from continental Europe, there have been Romani families and communities living in the UK. Romani, spoken by many Romanies in the UK, is a language with movement at its core. It is a mixed language that has picked up influences wherever the Romanies have travelled, and so incorporates aspects of Indian, Greek, Persian, Slavic and Romance languages, creating a philological map of their wanderings north and west from, it is thought, the Indian subcontinent. In Britain and Ireland this is mixed with English and with elements from the language of Irish Travellers (known as Gamin, Shelta or Cant).

The Romani words for the months have fallen out of common use now, but records of the Welsh Romani month names exist, and these were possibly once used by Romani communities all over Britain. They show a pattern of deep connection to the land and the seasons, as well as to work and food.

The word for January, Iveskero, means 'month of the snows'. The name dates from before 'wagon time' – the time when the Romani started living in wagons – and from a period when they would travel by walking alongside their wagons, which carried the makings of simple tents. These were constructed from willow wands bent and pushed into the ground and then covered with serge, a thick woollen fabric. Snow would have meant great hardship, as well as a struggle to look after their beloved horses, which would have been covered in cloths stuffed with straw to keep the cold away.

Charm of the Month

Calennig and Coal
for New Year's Day

Some days are naturally more strongly invested with meaning than others and so have held particular weight when it comes to luck and charms, and 1st January is one of them, acting as a hopeful microcosm for the whole year. Charms have always lent a sense of control and security where little existed, or have been used to hold on to the special qualities of certain moments of the year. On New Year's Day throughout the British Isles, charms must be carried through doors to carry in luck for the year ahead. In the southeast of Wales, children carry from door to door an apple skewered with sticks, cloves and pieces of evergreens, thought to bring luck and prosperity, and in return they are given 'calennig' – New Year's gifts of pennies or sweets. Sometimes the apples are then placed on windowsills to bring the household good luck through the year. In Scotland and the north of England, 'first footing' relates to the first person through your door on New Year's Day. Ideally it should be a bachelor, and he must have been out of the house at midnight. He should bring coal, bread, a coin, a piece of greenery, salt or whisky over the threshold.

A Song for Burns Night

'Ae Fond Kiss'

Robert Burns

On Burns Night on 25th January, cullen skink, haggis and tatties followed by cranachan are eaten, and the poems and songs of Robert Burns are recited, to celebrate the life of the great Scottish poet. 'Ae Fond Kiss' is one of his most beautiful songs and was written after his final meeting with his adored friend Mrs Agnes McLehose, known to her friends as Nancy, on her leaving Scotland to attempt a reconciliation with her estranged husband in Jamaica.

Ae   fond   kiss,   and   then   we   sev - er!   Ae   fare -

weel, al - as   for - ev   er,   Deep in   heart - wrung   tears I'll

pledge thee,   War - ing   sighs   and   groans   I'll   wage   thee.

Who shall say that Fortune grieves him,
While the star of hope she leaves him?
Me, nae cheerful twinkle lights me;
Dark despair around benights me.

I'll ne'er blame my partial fancy,
Naething could resist my Nancy;
But to see her was to love her;
Love but her, and love for ever.

Had we never lov'd sae kindly,
Had we never lov'd sae blindly,
Never met – or never parted,
We had ne'er been broken-hearted.

Fare-thee-weel, thou first and fairest!
Fare-thee-weel, thou best and dearest!
Thine be ilka joy and treasure,
Peace, Enjoyment, Love and Pleasure!

Ae fond kiss, and then we sever!
Ae fareweel, alas, for ever!
Deep in heart-wrung tears I'll pledge thee,
Warring sighs and groans I'll wage thee.

Folk Song of the Month

'Here We Come A-Wassailing'

Traditional, arr. Richard Barnard

This is a traditional wassailing song for Twelfth Night.
There were two distinct types of wassailing. One involved
moving from door to door singing and carrying a wassail
bowl, and the other was held in orchards, singing to and
blessing the trees for a fruitful year ahead. It is the second
type that is now more widespread, the rise in community
orchards sparking a revival, so look out for one near you
on or around Twelfth Night.

Here we come a-was-sail-ing a-mong the leaves so green,

here we come a-was-sail-ing so fair___ to be seen. *Love and*

joy come to you and to you a was-sail too, and God

bless you and send___ you a hap-py New Year and God

send you a hap-py New Year!

Here we come a-wassailing among the leaves so green,
Here we come a-wassailing so fair to be seen.
Love and joy come to you
And to you a wassail too,
And God bless you and send you a happy New Year
And God send you a happy New Year!

Call up the master of the house, put on his golden ring,
Bring us all a glass of ale and better we shall sing.
Love and joy come to you ...

We have a little purse and it is made of leather skin,
We want a silver sixpence to line it well within.
Love and joy come to you ...

God bless the master of the house and bless the mistress too,
And all the little children that round the table go.
Love and joy come to you ...

Epiphany, Lidat and the Three Kings

Balthazar was the King of Ethiopia. A new and bright star appeared in the sky, as had been foretold in the Star Prophecy: a prediction of the coming of a new Messiah. And so Balthazar gathered myrrh, the precious resin of the small thorny tree *Commiphora myrrha*, which grows in eastern and northern Ethiopia, and set off for Bethlehem with two other great kings – Caspar and Melchior – to pay their respects.

Rastafarians celebrate the birth of Christ, who they believe was Black, on 7th January, and call it Lidat, which means 'birthday' in Amharic, the main language of Ethiopia. Rastafari is intricately connected to Christianity but based upon a particular reading of the Bible that centres on its many mentions of Ethiopia, including its role as the 'promised land'. The Ethiopian Orthodox Church is after all one of the oldest churches in the world: Christianity has existed in Ethiopia since AD 330. Rastafari itself is a young religion, originating among impoverished African–Jamaican communities in the 1930s, its Africa-centric vision emerging partly as a reaction to British colonialism and as a way of reclaiming an African identity lost through slavery. Rastas believe that the Bible was originally written in Amharic and is an authentic account of early Black history and Black Africans' place as God's favoured people, the Israelites, but that this original meaning has been warped by mistranslation to deny Black Africans their true history.

This date of 7th January is in tune with the Julian calendar followed by the older Orthodox churches, but Rastas do not insist that this was the actual date of Jesus' birth (merely rejecting the date of the 25th December, which they consider a later construct to convert midwinter-worshipping pagans to Christianity). They do, however, consider this as the date upon which the Magi visited Jesus. A feast is prepared, children are given simple presents and they play games. The main decoration is that of the manger with the three Magi, including the Ethiopian king paying homage to the young Black Messiah.

Folk Story of the Month

The Farmer and the Boggart

The first Monday after Epiphany is Plough Monday. This was the traditional start of the English agricultural year and the day when work resumed after Christmas. Here is a very old tale said to originate in Lincolnshire, about a farmer ploughing and tilling his land, and outwitting a boggart – a malevolent spirit – in the process.

There was once a strong, handsome, hardworking farmer. The harvests were good for several years, and he saved up a little money so that when the fallow field alongside his farm came up for sale, he bought it. That night, he called to his wife, 'I am so happy to own the new field. We shall get a good crop this year.'

They were both shocked to hear a low, growly voice say, 'But it ain't yours, is it?' There, next to the fire, was a boggart – squat, hairy and strongly built. He told them that the field belonged to him, and that it had produced no crops for many years because the farmer wouldn't give him his fair share. Now, our farmer was canny and knew that a deal had to be made, so he asked the boggart what he required. 'I own the field, and you do the work,' said the boggart, 'so we should split the crop half and half.' 'Deal,' said the farmer. 'What do you want to take the first year then? The tops or the bottoms?' The boggart laughed as if it was obvious. 'Why, I'll take the tops, of course!'

The next day the farmer went out and sowed his field with turnips. At harvest time the boggart came to collect his half and the farmer presented him with a cartful of turnip tops. The boggart was furious, but the farmer reminded him of their deal and said, 'What will you have next year?' 'Why the bottoms, of course!' shouted the boggart. The farmer sowed his field with barley. Come harvest time, when the boggart came to collect his share the farmer presented him with a field full of stubble. The boggart stamped and raged and then stomped off away from the field, knowing he was beaten. He was never seen again.

Wolf Moon | Stay Home Moon
Moon After Yule

January's moon has several old names: Wolf Moon, from the time wolves howled particularly loudly to their packs through January nights; Stay Home Moon, a sensible idea in the cold and the frost and with all those wolves about; and Moon after Yule, which was given to the first full moon after the winter solstice.

When the full moon rises, it will be bright and bluish, but it will illuminate very few nocturnal creatures. Almost all stay home this month, tucking themselves away to survive the cold.

The wolf's close relative the fox is one of the few that do not hibernate. It picks its way on moonlit January nights through stubbly fields and down chilly streets to find a meal, or calls in unearthly cries for its mate, just as the wolves would have done hundreds of years ago.

A Song for January's Full Moon

'The Fox and the Goose'

Traditional, arr. Richard Barnard

This song follows a wily fox out on a chilly moonlit night. It started life as a 15th-century English poem and then made its way across the Atlantic to become a popular bluegrass song, albeit with a different tune to the original. This is closer to the old English version.

The fox went out on a winter night
And he prayed to the moon to give him light,
For he had no coal or candlelight
To guide him to the town-o...

The false fox came upon a croft
And there he stalked the geese so soft
For he had been here so fearful oft
When he had come to town-o...

He took a goose fast by the neck
And threw it quick behind his back.
The other geese began to quack
But he wouldn't lay it down-o...

The good man came out with his flail
And smote the fox upon the tail,
'Please come no more unto our hall
To bear our geese away-o,
way-o, way-o...'

The false fox ran back to his den
And there he was all merry then,
His wife and whelps could eat again
And chew upon the bones-o...

The fox went out on a winter night and he prayed to the moon to give him light,_____ for he had no coal or candle-light to guide him to the town - o, town - o, town-o_____ for he had no coal or candle-light to guide him to the town - o._____

17

A Sea Shanty for January
'Hieland Laddie'

For hundreds of years whaling was a huge part of the Scottish economy, with men setting off in whaleboats from the east-coast ports of Dundee and Peterhead to catch bowhead whales off Greenland in unimaginably cold, harsh and dangerous conditions. Happily, ever since the hunting of blue and humpback whales was banned globally in 1966 and a moratorium on commercial whaling took effect in 1986, the population has recovered significantly.

Shanties were working songs, from a time when human muscle had to do what steam and oil did later. The shanties kept men working together in time as they hauled and heaved on the various ropes and pumps on a merchant sailing vessel. Each shanty had a different use.

This is a 'walkaway' shanty for a continual hauling action, requiring a line of men to hold a rope and walk backwards while hauling on it. They would run back to the start of the line when they ran out of space. Such shanties generally had long choruses suited to the action.

There was a lad-die came from Scot-land, Hie-land lad-die, Bon-nie lad-die!

Bon-nie lad-die from fair Scot-land, me bon-nie Hie-land lad-die O!

Way, hay an' a-way we go, Hie-land lad-die! Bon-nie lad-die!

Way, hay an' a-way we go, me bon-nie Hie-land lad-die O!

Where have ye been when I looked for ye,
Heiland laddie, bonnie laddie?
Where have ye been when I looked for ye,
Me bonnie Hieland laddie O?
Way, hay an' away we go,
Hieland laddie! Bonnie laddie!
Way, hay an' away we go,
Me bonnie Hieland laddie O!

Joined a ship and went a-sailin'
Heiland laddie! Bonnie laddie!
Sailed far north and went a-whalin'
Me bonnie Hieland laddie O!
Way, hay...

Bound away to Iceland cold
Heiland laddie! Bonnie laddie!
Found much ice but not much gold
Me bonnie Hieland laddie O!
Way, hay...

I'll be glad when I get hame
Heiland laddie! Bonnie laddie!
I'll give up this whalin' game
Me bonnie Hieland laddie O!
Way, hay...

Soon be homeward bound to Scotland
Heiland laddie! Bonnie laddie!
Homeward bound to bonnie Scotland
Me bonnie Hieland laddie O!
Way, hay...

February

The Naming of February

Gearran (Scots Gaelic) | *Februar* (Scots/Ulster Scots)
Feabhra (Irish Gaelic) | *Toshiaght-arree* (Manx)
Chwefror (Welsh) | *Hwevrer* (Cornish)
Févri (Jèrriais) | *Bita kaulo munthos* (Romani)

At first glance it seems as if the languages of the British Isles have very little agreement over the naming of February, but, in fact, most of them have origins in the Latin name for the month, *Februarius*, which in itself arises from *februum*, meaning 'purification' (this is often the month of Lent and fasting, though not every year). If you say the Welsh Chwefror and the Cornish Hwevrer aloud, the similarities become clearer. However, the Scots Gaelic Gearran takes a different route this month – *gear an* means 'short month', which, of course, this is. Manx, likewise, goes its own way, as *toshiaght* means 'start' or 'beginning', and *arree* means 'spring' which is a hopeful and optimistic thought.

The Romani name for the month is Bita kaulo munthos – 'little black month'. This name must be a reference to the fact that this is the last of the dark months of winter, when the daylight hours are very short. An alternative Romani name for February is Kaulay Staur Kurkay, which means 'dark four weeks'. The root *kaul*, meaning 'black', comes up again and again in their language for words meaning 'Romani', including *kaulesko* ('of a Romani man') and *kauliako* ('of a Romani woman'), presumably referring to the dark skin and hair the Romani sometimes have, a pointer to their probable Indian ancestry. Already in February the Romanies would be back on the trail that took them around the harvests and through the seasons of wild flowers, crops, crafting and gatherings. The travelling year had begun.

Brigid's Way for St Brigid's Day

The first day of February is St Brigid's Day, a day of two women: one goddess and one saint, one from Ireland's pagan past and one from its Christian past. The goddess Brigid was one of the Tuatha Dé Danann, Ireland's mythical ancient race of gods. She was a healer, a poet and a smith, and is associated with spring, wells and fertility. She is also strongly associated with Imbolc, the Gaelic festival marking the end of winter and the beginning of early spring, which falls on 1st February. Imbolc means 'in the belly' and falls as lambing begins.

Brigid's Christian counterpart, St Brigid of Kildare, who was born in the 5th century and shares many of the same attributes, is one of the three patron saints of Ireland, along with Patrick and Columba. Her own feast day falls on the same day as Imbolc. Have their identities merged over the centuries or were they always – as some would have it – one and the same? It has been argued that Christian monks may have taken the goddess's attributes and grafted on the name of the saint in order to make use of the cult of Brigid in spreading the new religion through Ireland.

Either way, many people are now ready to turn back and embrace both aspects of Brigid, and this has led to the creation of a new pilgrimage based on ancient pilgrim paths and wells, Brigid's Way. It begins at St Brigid's birthplace at Faughart, in Co. Louth, and finishes in Kildare town, where Brigid founded a monastery. The 146-km route takes in holy wells dedicated to Brigid, as well as the Cuchulainn Stone, the Hill of Slane, the Hill of Tara and Brigid's Fire Temple, where nuns kept a flame burning until the suppression of the monasteries in the 16th century (and where the tradition was resurrected by the Brigidine Sisters in 1993). The ancient sites form a cross in the landscape, echoing the shape of St Brigid's Cross, an offset cross that is woven from rushes and placed over doorways and windows to protect against harm.

A Chinese New Year Story for February

The Great Race

Chinese New Year (which falls in January or February) is the most important celebration of the year in China and many other Asian countries, and is also widely celebrated around the world, including in the UK and Ireland.

The 12 Chinese zodiac signs are represented by animals in this order: Rat, Ox, Tiger, Rabbit, Dragon, Snake, Horse, Goat, Monkey, Rooster, Dog and Pig. Each animal in turn – combined with an element – rules the character of the year, and newborn babies will take on the characteristics of their year's animal.

The Jade Emperor – the gentle and caring ruler of the gods in Chinese mythology – asked all of the animals to gather for a race to celebrate his birthday. The first 12 animals would be given a place as his guards at the heavenly gate for ever more, and so all of the animals were keen to do their best.

The race was across a great wide river, and the quick-witted rat noticed the ox, steady and dependable, and leapt upon his ear as he started to swim the river. The ox didn't notice, and carried the rat over. The rat leapt from his ear and crossed the finish line first, but the ox, being kind-natured, happily took second place. Next came the tiger, surging confidently out of the water, followed by the rabbit, who had skilfully hopped upon a log and drifted across. The good-natured dragon was next, having slowed down when he had noticed the rabbit on the log, and having used his breath to sweep the rabbit across. Clever snake and lively horse came next, followed by the shy goat and the clever monkey, the courageous rooster and the loyal dog. Finally, puffing over the water, came the generous and easy-going pig. He had become hungry and stopped to eat but had then fallen asleep. The emperor chuckled and announced the race concluded.

Folk Song of the Month

'The Lion's Den
(The Lady of Carlisle)'

Traditional, arr. Richard Barnard

The Lion dancers are one of the main attractions at any Chinese New Year celebration. Two dancers make up a lion, with one taking the highly decorated head and the other playing the back half, like a pantomime horse. The vigorous and energetic movements come from martial arts, and the music is a loud drum beat, with cymbals and gongs. Troupes will visit local homes and shops and take part in the traditional custom of Cai Qing ('plucking the greens'). An envelope stuffed with greenery such as lettuce is left out for the lion, as well as a red envelope full of money for the troupe. The lion eats and spits out the green envelope and keeps the red one.

To celebrate the Lion dancers that grace every Chinese New Year celebration, here is an English traditional song that mentions both lions and tigers, and an unusual method for finding your true love.

Down in Carlisle there lived a lady,
She was a beauty, fine and gay.
She was resolved to live a lady;
No man on earth would her betray.
She'd only choose a man of honour,
A man of honour and high degree,
And then there came two handsome brothers
This fair young lady for to see.

The first of them a bold sea captain
Belonging to the colonel's corps.
The other was a brave lieutenant
On board the Tiger man-of-war.
She ordered coachmen to get ready
And to the tower they drove, all three,
And there they'd spend one single hour,
The lions and tigers for to see.

The lions and tigers gave such a roaring
And in the den she threw her fan,
Saying 'Which of you, to gain a lady,
Will return my fan again?'
First up spoke the colonel's captain
And said, 'Your offer I can't approve.'
But then spoke loud, the poor lieutenant:
'My life I'll venture for your love.'

And in the den he bravely entered
With lions and tigers fierce and grim
But when they saw his blood was royal
They never touched a hair on him.
And when she saw him come before her,
And no harm to him was done
She laid her head upon his bosom
Saying, 'Here's the prize that you have won.'

Folk Story of the Month

The Nodding Tiger

A poor old lady called Widow T'ang lived with her son in a little one-room shack. They had nothing, but every day the son would go out and cut wood to sell to their neighbours, and in this way they scraped by. One morning he went out, waving a cheery goodbye, but by late evening he hadn't returned. His mother paced and fretted, and in the morning a neighbour set off to look for him. The neighbour hadn't gone far up the mountain when he came across the son's bloodied and torn clothes, and he knew that a tiger had carried him away.

Widow T'ang was beside herself with grief, but rather than sit weeping she walked to the city, stood in front of the magistrate and demanded that the tiger be brought to justice. 'I have lost my son, and have nobody to provide and care for me in my old age. The tiger must be punished!' she said.

The magistrate took pity on her and sent his men out into the forest to hunt for the tiger, but when they found his cave he did not attack them, he simply nodded his head, as if he knew he had done wrong. The men put a strong chain around his neck and led him down the mountain and to the magistrate.

The magistrate – feeling a little silly – asked the tiger if he had eaten Widow T'ang's son. The tiger nodded his head. And so the magistrate said, 'This old woman has nobody to support her. Will you promise to feed her and care for her?' The tiger nodded, so the chain was removed from his neck and he walked peacefully out of the courtroom and back to his cave.

The old woman was furious – she had wanted vengeance, and what good was a tiger's word to her? But the very next day she woke to find a freshly killed deer outside her door, which she butchered and sold at the market. And the tiger kept his promise, delivering food and gifts every week. The old woman grew rich, and in the evenings the tiger would come to the shack and purr as she stroked his fur. They became the best of friends, and the tiger looked after her for the rest of her life.

A Song for Valentine's Day

'Tomorrow Is St Valentine's Day'

William Shakespeare

This bawdy tale of love, lust and very swift rejection serves as a warning to maids not to come to bed too readily, Valentine's Day or no. It is sung by Ophelia in *Hamlet*, after he rejects her, but is thought to be an older song.

The young man rose and donned his clothes,
And dupped the chamber door,
Let in the maid that out, a maid,
Never departed more.

Quoth she, Before you tumbled me,
You promised me to wed,
That would I have done, by yonder sun,
If thou hadst not come to my bed.

By Gis and by Saint Charity,
Away and fie for shame.
Young men will do it, when they come to it,
By cock, they are to blame.

'Hooraw for the Black Ball Line'

A song for the 'little black month', and for the snow and ice that often come with it. The Black Ball Line was a series of packet ships that ran between Liverpool and New York from 1816 until around 1850, keeping a pretty much regular timetable from 1822 with two sailings per month in all weathers. It was the first line of sailing ships to take passengers and carried many hopeful migrants to the New World to seek their fortunes in the gold mines. It was named after its flag, a black ball on a red background.

This is a 'capstan' shanty. Heavy jobs such as raising the anchor used a capstan, a sort of vertical barrel with spokes that the sailors walked around, one pushing on each spoke, which would gradually pull in the anchor or other rope. These jobs being particularly lengthy and laborious, many capstan shanties have long verses and grand choruses, for joining in, though this one in particular doesn't follow that pattern.

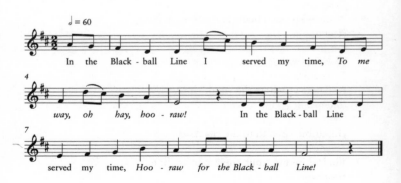

Blackball ships are good and true,
To me way, oh hay, hooraw!
They are the ships for me and you,
Hooraw for the Blackball Line!

I've sailed that line full many a time
To me way...
It's there I wasted all me prime
Hooraw...

Just take a ship to Liverpool
To me way...
To Liverpool that packet school
Hooraw...

Yankee sailors you'll see there
To me way...
With red-topped boots and short-cut hair
Hooraw...

The ship will go through ice an' snow
To me way...
And take ye where the winds don't blow
Hooraw...

Oh, drink a health to the Blackball Line
To me way...
Their ships are stout, their men are fine
Hooraw...

Snow Moon | Ice Moon
Storm Moon

Even if there is not enough snow to justify the medieval moon name Snow Moon, the February full moon will light up snowy expanses across meadows, woodlands and river banks as snowdrop time reaches its peak. Snowdrops began popping their heads out of the cold ground in January, proving that even though the ground is still bare and hard with frost, spring is straining at the bit. The names Ice Moon and Storm Moon also hint at an understandable preoccupation with this month's weather in the past, when heating meant a few logs on the fire to fend off the deep chill of February.

A Song for February's Full Moon

'The Moon Shined on
My Bed Last Night'

Traditional, arr. Richard Barnard

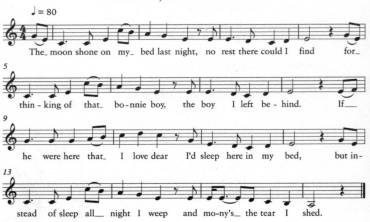

♩ = 80

The moon shone on my bed last night, no rest there could I find for thinking of that bonnie boy, the boy I left behind. If he were here that I love dear I'd sleep here in my bed, but instead of sleep all night I weep and mony's the tear I shed.

This beautiful Scottish ballad finds a young woman lamenting marrying for money. In some versions she sets out to find her true love, and hang the consequences. Alas, in this one she simply languishes in the moonlight, broken-hearted.

The moon shone on my bed last night,
No rest there could I find
For thinking of that bonnie boy,
The boy I left behind.
If he were here that I love dear
I'd sleep here in my bed,
But instead of sleep all night I weep
And mony's the tear I shed.

For an auld man came a-courting me
He sought me for his bride.
My parents they advised me so
To have him by my side.
He had a little money,
It was all they would endure,
But I'd rather go a-roving
With my roving bonnie boy.

For some speak ill of my true love
And mony speak ill of me,
But I let them all say whit they will
I'd rather his company.
If he were here that I love dear
I'd sleep here in my bed,
But instead of sleep all night I weep
And mony's the tear I shed.

March

The Naming of March

Màrt (Scots Gaelic) | *Mairch* (Scots/Ulster Scots)
Márta (Irish Gaelic) | *Mayrnt* (Manx)
Mawrth (Welsh) | *Meurth* (Cornish)
Mar (Jèrriais) | *Bavalyakero* (Romani)

This month there is universal agreement between the languages of the British Isles. All hark back to *Martius*, the first month of the Roman calendar, which itself comes from Mars, the Roman god of war and of agriculture, this being his month. March's position as the first month of the year was widespread, and 25th March was considered the first day of the year in England until 1752.

March is blustery and blowy, the cheery daffodils are battered (they don't seem to mind) and the tree branches with their new buds are being swished to and fro.

Wind is pretty universally hated within the Romani community even now, particularly for its ability to overturn a wagon once it really gets strong. Even blustery gusts make wagon- and tent-living rather uncomfortable, as well as interfering with the functions of living out-of-doors. So this is another month named after pesky weather, which is so immediate to those living close to nature. The Romani word *bavalesko* means 'of the wind' and *yakengeriengo* means 'of the clocks', so perhaps Bavalyakero means something like 'wind time'.

The Story of St Patrick

St Patrick started life as Maewyn Succat, a boy from a rich family living an easy life in Roman Britain in the 5th century, somewhere near Cumbria. But when he was about 16 years old the path of his life dramatically changed: Irish pirates raiding his family's estate captured him and carried him away across the Irish Sea, where he was enslaved and forced to herd and tend sheep.

Ireland was at that time ruled by many kings and by a priestly caste of druids, who worshipped an ancient race of heroic fighting and feasting gods called the Tuatha Dé Danann. It was a loose, earthy and hedonistic religion, its stories passed by word of mouth. Maewyn used his time in the fields devoutly praying and finding a faith in God, as well as observing the Irish way of life and learning the Irish language. After six years of captivity he fled from his master and sailed home, where he studied Christianity.

Acting on a vision, he returned as a Christian missionary to Ireland, where he used his understanding of the Irish culture to convert people from their old pagan ways; famously, he used the shamrock to illustrate the Holy Trinity. He came into conflict with the druid priests and Irish kings, and even apocryphally met with and attempted to convert the very god-warriors themselves. Despite having no luck in that respect, he went on to successfully convert and baptise thousands of Irish people, and is credited with bringing Christianity to Ireland. Hailed as the 'Apostle of Ireland', he referred to himself in writings as Patricius, which means 'father of the citizens'.

Patrick is thought to have died on 17th March, and this became his feast day. Over time he has become particularly associated with Catholic Ireland, with the colour green – which in the Irish flag represents Catholics – and with Irish national identity. Wherever the Irish diaspora has settled in large numbers around the world, St Patrick's Day is a day to gather, drink, sing and celebrate all things Irish.

Charm of the Month

Four-Leaf Clover

The association of four-leaf clovers with luck may have arisen from their relative scarcity: only about one in five thousand clovers will have the extra leaf, so those with the extra one are a bit special and worth tucking into your pocket when you need luck on your side.

It is said that you will only find one when you're not looking (though once you have, keep looking: the same plant is likely to produce more). They were carried by Welsh Celts as a charm against evil spirits, and there are records of them being used all over the British Isles. However, they are most associated with Ireland and with St Patrick. When they are not representing the Father, the Son and the Holy Ghost, the three leaves represent faith, hope and love, with the exceptional fourth adding luck. It is said that there are more four-leaf clovers in Ireland than there are in the rest of the British Isles, thus accounting for the 'luck of the Irish'.

A Song for St Patrick's Day
'Paddy's Green Shamrock Shore'

Traditional

Many Irish folk songs are about leaving Ireland and then longing for it, sometimes by enforced transportation at the hands of the harsh British penal system, sometimes economic emigration across the Atlantic to escape poverty and famine. This song is in the latter tradition, but is one of the more jolly examples: everyone arrives safe and excited to seek their fortune. If it weren't for the longing for sweet Liza and those shamrock-coloured shores this could almost count as a happy ending.

From Derry quay we sailed away on the twenty-third of May We were boarded by a pleasant crew, bound for Americay Fresh water then we did take on, five thousand gallons or more In case we'd run short going to New York far away from the shamrock shore.

So fare thee well, sweet Liza dear and likewise Derry town
And twice farewell to my comrade boys that dwell on that sainted ground
If fortune it should favour me, and I to have money in store
I'll come back and I'll wed the wee lassie I left on Paddy's green shamrock shore.

At twelve o'clock we came in sight of famous Mullin Head
And Innistrochlin to the right stood out on the ocean's bed.
A grander sight ne'er met my eyes than e'er I saw before
Than the sun going down 'twixt sea and sky far away from the shamrock shore.

We sailed three weeks, we were all seasick, not a man on board was free
We were all confined unto our bunks and no-one to pity poor me.
No father kind nor mother dear to lift up my head, which was sore
Which made me think more on the lassie I left on Paddy's green shamrock shore.

We safely reached the other side after fifteen and twenty days,
We were taken as passengers by a man and led round in six different ways,
We each of us drank a parting glass, in case we'd meet no more
And we drank a health to old Ireland and Paddy's green shamrock shore.

Leprechauns and Green for St Patrick's Day

On 17th March throughout Ireland and in areas of the UK with large Irish populations, St Patrick's Day parades fill the streets with green hats and clothes and Guinness. The colour of Ireland was not always green – it was once a cool light blue, as depicted in early Irish flags, reflecting the colours worn by St Patrick. But from the Irish Rebellion of 1641 onwards, green flags and clothing started to be carried and worn by Irish revolutionaries, one important element in distinguishing Ireland from the UK and from the colours of the British flag. As Ireland is so verdant that it is known as the Emerald Isle, green certainly feels like its colour.

A good proportion of St Patrick's Day revellers will go a step further and dress as leprechauns. Leprechauns are the 'little people' in Irish mythology, fairy shoemakers. One origin story has them as the diminished remnants of the Tuatha Dé Danann, the pagan, gods race that ruled pre-Christian Ireland – once they were no longer worshipped, they shrank in size. The word leprechaun is thought possibly to originate from the Old Irish *luchorpán*, in which *lú* means 'small' and *cor* means 'body'.

Cunning and mischievous, they love to trick humans and to hoard gold. The gold dates from the invasion of Ireland by the Danes, who are said to have entrusted their plundered treasure to the leprechauns, who hid it in crocks all around Ireland. You will find a crock at the end of a rainbow, but if you come across a leprechaun and quiz him, he is bound to tell you where it is, just so long as you never take your eyes off him – if you do he will vanish in a moment.

Folk Story of the Month

The Red Handkerchief

Here is a story that tells you all you need to know about leprechauns: how to discover where their gold is hidden, and how they will most probably get the better of you anyway.

A young man was walking along by moonlight when he heard a shriek. Being a fit and brave fellow, he ran to see what was afoot. Hanging from a blackthorn bush was a little man all dressed in green. At the base of the bush was a hammer and a pair of shoes. What luck! The man had found a leprechaun.

'What are you doing up there?' he said to the leprechaun.

'None of your business,' answered the leprechaun crossly. 'Just get me down!'

Now the man knew that as soon as he let go, the leprechaun would vanish, so he unhooked him but then kept a firm grip.

'Where is your pot of gold?' he demanded, looking the leprechaun firmly in the eye (because this is the way to make a leprechaun relinquish his treasure). The leprechaun sighed and pointed to another blackthorn bush.

While this was excellent news, our man couldn't dig it up with his bare hands. 'I will need to go and fetch my spade. How will I find the tree when I return?' he asked the leprechaun.

'I don't know and I don't care,' was the cross reply.

'Aha, I know! I will tie my red handkerchief to the tree and then I will be able to find it. But before I release you, you must promise that you will not touch it or move it while I am gone.'

'Yes, yes, I promise. Now let me go,' said the leprechaun.

And so the man let go of the leprechaun (who instantly vanished), tied his handkerchief to the tree and set off for home.

The next day he set off early to claim his fortune. He immediately spotted his tree, tied with the handkerchief, and started digging. But then he spotted another tree up ahead, also tied with a red handkerchief, and another, and another. In fact, every single blackthorn tree sported its own red handkerchief. The man knew then that the leprechaun had outwitted him, and he picked up his spade and headed for home.

Folk Song of the Month

'The Wearing of the Green'

Traditional, arr. Richard Barnard

This song charts a little of the history of the colour green, Ireland and St Patrick's Day. The Society of Irishmen, formed in the wake of the French Revolution to bring about an Irish national government with equal representation, adopted green as their colour. This is about the repression of those wearing it.

Oh, Paddy dear, and did you hear the news that's going round?
The shamrock is forbid by law to grow on Irish ground!
No more to keep Saint Patrick's Day, his colours can't be seen
For there's a cruel law against the Wearing of the Green.

Oh, I met with Napper Tandy and he took me by the hand
And he said, 'How's dear old Ireland and how does she stand?'
'She's the most distressful country that ever yet was seen,
For they're hanging men and women
for the Wearing of the Green.'

And if the colour we must wear is England's cruel red
Let it remind us of the blood that Ireland has shed.
You may pull the shamrock from your hat and throw it on the sod
But you will see it take root there, though underfoot 'tis trod.

When laws can stop the blades of grass for growing as they grow
And when the leaves in summertime their colour dare not show
Then I will change the colour that I wear in my cáibín,
But 'til that day, please God, I'll stick to Wearing of the Green.

March's Full Moon

Plough Moon | Wind Moon
Lenten Moon | Chaste Moon

Finally spring feels unstoppable and the landscape beneath this month's full moon is easing its way out of winter's grip, with banks of pale wild daffodils swaying in the March breezes and dots of blossom visible under its silvery light. Throughout the year we will see a series of moon names that reference big seasonal jobs, and the Plough Moon is the first of these, perhaps suggesting that the light of the full moon allowed people to carry on ploughing well into the evening. Farming and gardening begin in earnest this month, often in gusty conditions, as the name Wind Moon suggests.

The name Lenten Moon for March's full moon partially corresponds with Lent, the traditional period of fasting that precedes Easter, and the Celtic name Chaste Moon may also allude to Lent's constraints. But the word itself originates in the Old English word *lencten*, which means 'spring' and is in reference to the lengthening days, which are hard to ignore as this month we reach the equinox, when day and night are finally the same length.

A Song for March's Full Moon

'Ar Hyd y Nos'/ 'All Through the Night'

Traditional, arr. Richard Barnard

A Welsh lullaby written by John Ceiriog Hughes in the late 19th century, and understandably popular with Welsh male voice choirs, this is often sung for St David's Day, which falls on 1st March. It has been variously translated into English or given unrelated English words throughout its history, and the English version given here is not a direct translation of the Welsh original. It is based roughly on a version by Harold Boulton but with some lines brought a little closer in meaning to the Welsh version.

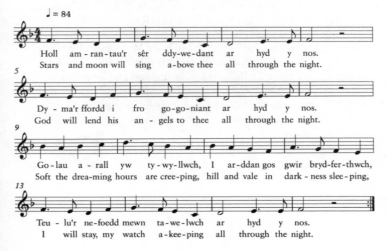

Holl am-ran-tau'r sêr ddy-we-dant ar hyd y nos.
Stars and moon will sing a-bove thee all through the night.

Dy - ma'r ffordd i fro go-go-niant ar hyd y nos.
God will lend his an - gels to thee all through the night.

Go-lau a - rall yw ty-wy-llwch, I ar-ddan gos gwir bryd-fer-thwch,
Soft the drea-ming hours are cree-ping, hill and vale in dark - ness slee-ping,

Teu - lu'r ne-foedd mewn ta-we-lwch ar hyd y nos.
I will stay, my watch a-kee-ping all through the night.

April

The Naming of April

Giblean (Scots Gaelic)
Apryle (Scots/Ulster Scots)
Aibreán (Irish Gaelic) | *Averil* (Manx)
Ebrill (Welsh) | *Ebryll* (Cornish) | *Avri* (Jèrriais)
Brishindeskero (Romani)

The *Fasti Praenestini* is an ancient Roman calendar
carved in marble, or at least the remains of it.
Only parts of January, March, April and December
survive, but it has left a tantalising clue as to the
origins of the name of this month. The Roman
month *Aprilis* is derived from *aperio*, 'to open', and
the *Fasti* has an idea as to why: 'Fruits and flowers
and animals and lands and seas do open' this month,
it says. Most of the names for April in the languages
of the British Isles appear to have originated with
Aprilis, with the possible exceptions of the Irish
Gaelic Aibreán and the Scots Gaelic Giblean, which
may come from *braon*, meaning 'drops of rain'.
The Romani name for the month means 'month
of the rains'.

A Jewish Tale for April

The Passover Seder

The Israelites were the slaves of ancient Egypt, and the people from whom modern Jews believe they are descended. They were subjected to cruelty and hard labour and forced to build the pyramids and to work in the fields. Moses went to the Pharaoh and asked him to set his people free, but the Pharaoh refused, so God rained ten plagues down upon Egypt. The first nine – in which water turned to blood, the Nile teemed with frogs, lice crawled over men and beasts, wild animals attacked, livestock were diseased, festering boils afflicted men and animals, hail fell, locusts swarmed, and three days of darkness spread over Egypt – failed to move the Pharaoh; the Israelites remained enslaved. Finally, God told the Israelites to sacrifice a lamb and to daub the blood on their doorways. He sent an angel of death to kill all of the first-born children in the land, but to pass over those with the blood mark. Overnight, every Egyptian first-born in the land was killed. The Pharaoh set the Israelites free and commanded them to leave immediately.

Passover, or Pesach, begins on the 15th day of the month of Nisan (which falls in March or April) and with the first Seder, which commemorates the exodus from Egypt of the Israelites. It is part ritualised meal, part retelling of the story, which Jews are obliged to repeat each year: it is thought that the Last Supper may have been a Passover Seder. Jews use a book known as the Haggadah, which means 'the telling', to guide them through the evening.

The Seder Plate is central to the telling. It contains six traditional items: Maror and Chazeret (bitter herbs, such as parsley or endives), for the bitter times the Israelites had endured; Zeroa (the shank bone of a lamb), for the sacrificial Paschal Lamb; Beitzah (an egg), for hope; Charoset (a paste of apples, nuts and wine), for the mortar the Israelites were forced to use to build ancient Egypt; and Karpas (parsley or a green vegetable), which is dipped in salted water and represents the Israelites' hard labour and tears. Matzah (unleavened bread) accompanies these six items, symbolising the fact that the Israelites had to leave so quickly that their bread did not have time to rise.

Charm of the Month

Coloured Eggs for Easter

Easter's association with eggs is one of the great threads that stretches from the present back into the ancient past. We know that eggs are partly associated with Easter because egg-free Lent created a backlog to be eaten, decorated and rolled down hills with joyful abandon on Easter Sunday. However, there may be far older, pagan associations connected to the feeling of rebirth and fertility that comes with the equinox and with moving out of the dark half of the year and into the light. Decorating eggs has a long and certainly pre-Christian tradition in Eastern Europe and Persia. The earliest record of it in the British Isles is in the 13th century, when King Edward I ordered 450 eggs to be decorated as Easter gifts, though the practice may well have been going on unrecorded for some time before that.

To decorate an egg, first make a small hole at the top and another at the bottom. Put your mouth to the top hole and blow the egg contents into a bowl (saving them for an eggy dish). Wash the egg through and then paint, felt-tip or stick designs on it. Give decorated eggs to friends and family as a symbol of this hopeful and expectant moment in the year.

A Song for Spring

'When Spring Comes In'

Traditional

This song is a simple and joyful celebration of this lovely moment in the year, when winter is finally relinquishing its grip.

When spring comes in the birds do sing the lambs do skip and the

bells do ring, While we en-joy their glor - ious charm so

no-ble and so gay oh the prim-rose blooms and the cow slip too the

vi-olets in their sweet re-tire, the ro - ses shi - ning through the briar and the

daff-o-downdillies that we ad-mire will die and fade a - way.

Young men and maidens will be seen,
On mountains high and meadows green,
They will talk of love and sport and play,
While these young lambs do skip away.
At night they homeward wend their way,
When evening stars appear.

Chorus:
Oh the primrose blooms and the cowslip too,
The violets in their sweet retire, the roses shining through the briar,
And the daffadowndillies that we admire will die and fade away.

The dairymaid to milking goes, her
blooming cheeks as red as a rose,
She carries her pail all on her arm so cheerful and so gay,
She milks, she sings, and the valleys ring,
The small birds on the branches there
sit listening to this lovely fair.
For she is her master's trust and care, she is the ploughman's joy.

Chorus

Folk Story of the Month

St George and the Dragon

The story of St George killing the dragon is a shining example of the mummers' – players who would perform for winter festivals – tales of battles between the forces of good and the devil. It is, of course, also St George's Day on the 23rd April. History tells us that St George never even set foot in England and that the following story was originally set in Cappadocia (modern Turkey), but legend still insists it all happened on Dragon Hill at Uffington in Oxfordshire. The flat top of this hillock has a patch where grass will not grow, the blood of the dragon being so poisonous that it still kills the grass all of these hundreds of years later.

There was once a town plagued by a dragon that ravaged the countryside, poisoning the fields and eating the livestock.

The townspeople were distraught, so they offered the dragon sacrifices. At first these were two sheep, each day; then a man and a sheep; and finally the youths of the town, drawn by lot and sent to die. One day this fate fell to the king's daughter.

The king offered the people all of his money to save her, but the people insisted that what was good enough for their children was good enough for her. The king's daughter was dressed as a bride and walked in a procession down to the dragon's lair.

St George was at that moment nearby, and when he saw the girl and heard the tale he vowed to protect her. When the dragon emerged to claim its meal, St George made the sign of the cross at it and then charged on his horse, wounding the dragon with his lance. St George shouted to the princess to throw him her girdle, and he then placed this around the dragon's neck, at which the dragon suddenly became calm and meekly followed them back into the town.

St George offered to slay the dragon if the townspeople converted to Christianity and were baptised, and surprisingly enough they agreed. He beheaded it with his sword and the townspeople were able to live in peace.

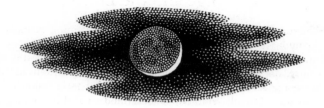

April's Full Moon

Budding Moon
New Shoots Moon | Seed Moon
Paschal Moon

The medieval names of the full moon often reference agricultural markers, and none more so than April's: Budding Moon, New Shoots Moon and Seed Moon, which neatly tell you everything you need to know about the atmosphere and thrust of this month. April is still, of course, the time for seed sowing, just as it would have been in medieval times. Under April's full moon the countryside is no longer bare with dark twigs and stems. A soft fuzz of brightest green covers the black branches, and fluffs of blackthorn and damson blossom are appearing, bright pinpricks of white in the moonlight. The nights are shortening, lightening and losing their sharp chill, and the seeds that fell to the ground last autumn are finding warming earth and moisture and are starting to germinate. This moon is also the Paschal Moon, the first full moon after the spring equinox and the date by which Easter is calculated.

A Song for April's Full Moon

'The Rising of the Moon'

By John Keegan Casey, arr. Richard Barnard

The role of the moon in this evocative Irish ballad was to act as a secret signal, something all those in the know could look out for, to rise in unified rebellion: 'the pikes must be together at the rising of the moon'. It was written by John Keegan Casey in 1866 about the doomed 1798 Rebellion, a battle between the United Irishmen and the British Army.

Oh, come tell me, Sean O'Farrell, tell me why you hurry so?
'Hush, my bhuachaill, hush and listen,' and his eyes were all aglow
'I bear orders from the captain, get you ready quick and soon
With your pike upon your shoulder at the rising of the moon.
At the rising of the moon, at the rising of the moon
With your pike upon your shoulder at the rising of the moon.'

Tell me, tell me, Sean O'Farrell, where the gathering is to be?
'Near the old spot by the river, right well known to you and me.'
One last word, the signal token? 'Whistle out the marching tune
For our pikes must be together by the rising of the moon.
By the rising of the moon, by the rising of the moon
For our pikes must be together by the rising of the moon.'

Out from many mud-walled cabins, eyes
were looking through the night
Many manly hearts were beating for the blessed morning light.
A cry was heard along the river, like some banshee's mournful croon
And a thousand pikes were flashing by the rising of the moon.
By the rising of the moon, by the rising of the moon
And a thousand pikes were flashing by the rising of the moon.

All along the shining river one dark mass of men was seen
And above them in the night sky flew their own immortal green.
Death to every foe and traitor! Onward, strike the marching tune
And hurrah my boys for freedom, 'tis the rising of the moon.
'Tis the rising of the moon, 'tis the rising of the moon
And hurrah my boys for freedom, 'tis the rising of the moon.

A Sea Shanty for April

'A Wife in Every Port'

A song for the month of the rains. While wind and gales are frequently mentioned in sea shanties, rain is not, presumably because a bit of rain is nothing when you have massive waves crashing over the deck and soaking you through. But here rain gets a mention, perhaps just to underline how very hard our sailor has worked to get back to his lassie. Despite these heroics and as the title suggests, no one comes out of this tale looking good, though likewise the outcome might well suit all quite nicely.

This appears to be a shanty for heaving jobs, possibly used for capstan and pump. As it is a 'homeward bounder' (a song that mentions home) it might have been an 'anchor song', for keeping time when raising or lowering the anchor.

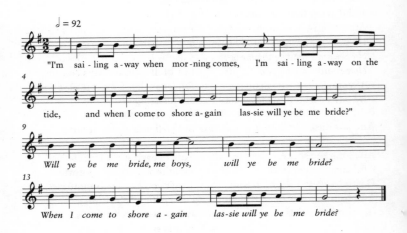

♩ = 92

"I'm sai-ling a-way when mor-ning comes, I'm sai-ling a-way on the tide, and when I come to shore a-gain las-sie will ye be me bride?"

Will ye be me bride, me boys, will ye be me bride?

When I come to shore a-gain las-sie will ye be me bride?

'Laddie, I will wait for you
As long as all me life.
Laddie, I will wait for you
I'll be a sailor's wife.'
I'll be a sailor's wife, me boys,
I'll be a sailor's wife
Laddie, I will wait for you
I'll be a sailor's wife.

The sun it shone and wind it blew
And the ship sailed out to sea,
When she caught the eye of a soldier lad
Standing on the quay.
Standing on the quay, me boys,
Standing on the quay
She caught the eye of a soldier lad
Standing on the quay.

The wind it blew and the cannons roared
and driving was the rain,
After twelve long months at sea
He was homeward bound again.
Homeward bound again, me boys,
Homeward bound again
After twelve long months at sea
He was homeward bound again.

And there he met her at the docks
With a baby in her arms
Saying, 'I am sorry, sailor lad,
But I fell for a soldier's charms.'
Fell for a soldier's charms, me boys,
Fell for a soldier's charms
I am sorry, sailor lad,
But I fell for a soldier's charms.

'Don't you fret me bonnie lass'
Was the sailor's bold retort,
'Don't you fret me bonnie lass,
I've a wife in every port!'
Wife in every port, me boys,
Wife in every port
Don't you fret me bonnie lass,
I've a wife in every port!

May

The Naming of May

Cèitean (Scots Gaelic) | *Mey* (Scots/Ulster Scots)
Bealtaine (Irish Gaelic)
Boaldyn/Toshiaght souree (Manx) | *Mai* (Welsh)
Me (Cornish) | *Mai* (Jèrriais)
Parne-kareskero/ Bakichengero (Romani)

There are several distinct origins of the names used for this
month around the British Isles. Several – just like 'May' – are
clearly derived from the ancient Roman month name *Maius*,
named either after Maia, the goddess of spring and fertility,
or after the word for elders, *maiores*, as suggested by Ovid.
But Irish Gaelic Bealtaine and Manx Boaldyn are derived
from Beltanē (or Beltaine), the Gaelic May Day festival held
on 1st May, roughly halfway between the spring equinox
and the summer solstice. Beltane was a fire festival and the
fires lit that day were thought to have magical and protective
qualities – the name Beltane may come from Celtic *belo-tenia*
meaning 'bright fire'. Beltane marks the start of summer,
and the day that cattle were driven out to summer pastures.

Cèitean in Scots Gaelic means 'beginning', and a second
name for May in Manx is Toshiaght Souree, *toshiaght*
meaning 'beginning' and *souree* meaning 'summer'. May
marks the start of the months of growth.

The Romani named the month Parne-kareskero – 'month
of the hawthorn' – for the great froth of hawthorn blossom
that lines almost every field this month. May flower buds
were traditionally eaten and it was said that they prevented
illness for the rest of the year; perhaps they provided some
boost of vitamins that had been lacking in the diet over the
winter. In addition to Parne-kareskero, a second Romani
language name for the month is Bakichengero, which means
'month of the lambs'.

A Song for May Day

'Solidarity Forever'

Ralph Chaplin

1st May is International Workers' Day, more widely known as May Day, and is often the focus for demonstrations and marches: a celebration of labourers, workers and the unions that have helped strengthen their hand and improve working conditions. 'Solidarity Forever' was written in the US in 1915 by Ralph Chaplin in support of the American union movement but has been adopted as a union anthem across the world.

Is there aught we hold in common with the greedy parasite,
Who would lash us into serfdom and would crush us with his might?
Is there anything left to us but to organise and fight?
For the union makes us strong.

Chorus:
Solidarity forever,
Solidarity forever,
Solidarity forever,
Cause the union makes us strong.

All the world that's owned by idle drones is ours and ours alone.
We have laid the wide foundations; built it skyward stone by stone.
It is ours, not to slave in, but to master and to own.
While the union makes us strong.

Chorus

They have taken untold millions that they never toiled to earn,
But without our brain and muscle not a single wheel can turn.
We can break their haughty power, gain our freedom when we learn
That the union makes us strong.

Chorus

In our hands is placed a power greater than their hoarded gold,
Greater than the might of armies, multiplied a thousand-fold.
We can bring to birth a new world from the ashes of the old
For the union makes us strong.

A Charm for May

Primroses for the Fairies

Belief in fairies was strong throughout the British Isles well into the 19th century, from the *aos sìth* of Scotland and the *aos sí* of Ireland to the *tylwyth teg* of Wales. We now think of fairies as winged, delicate, harmless little creatures, but the fairies of old were very much earthbound, and their dark side was strong. While they could bring luck and blessings, they were also fickle and easily angered, as well as being not at all averse to a bit of child kidnapping or – possibly worse – swapping in 'changelings' for healthy children. Sources claim either the first three days of May or May Day Eve as the time when fairies' wicked tendencies were to the fore. (Despite the title, Shakespeare's *A Midsummer Night's Dream* – which has put about the idea that Midsummer is when the fairies and humans intermingle – is actually set on May Day Eve.) They could be expected to make a foray to at least steal some butter, if not your actual first-born. In *A Treasury of British Folklore*, Dee Dee Chainey writes that primroses have a particular power against fairies, and no fairies can pass them, so they should be scattered along the threshold during the first few days of this month.

Dressing Up in May

Robin Hood and the Green Man

The Green Man is the spirit of summer, the Oak King to winter's Holly King, picking up the reins as summer begins, or even fighting and killing the Holly King to allow the summer in. In some May celebrations he will appear as Jack-in-the-Green, Puck or Robin Goodfellow. But he is Robin Hood at Helston, in Cornwall, at the Hal-an-Tow, which is part of the Flora Day celebrations (usually held on 8th May, unless that is a Sunday or Monday, in which case it is held on the previous Saturday).

Some scholars have assumed that Robin Hood was a real human being, while others have put his legendary status down to something more pagan and supernatural: a summer lord and king of the greenwood, an outlaw spirit and a virile symbol of the growth, fertility and careless pleasure of the summer. Although it seems likely that he was a real woodland rebel, over the centuries he has blended into a combination of the two.

What we do know for certain is that Robin Hood was the subject of several ballads, which later were turned into plays that became central to early Tudor May Games, presumably due to the joy to be had hearing about an outlaw outwitting an oppressive ruling class. May Games occurred each year during the slight breathing space between the major agricultural jobs of early spring (ploughing and sowing) and summer (haymaking). Over time, such plays morphed into Morris dances, and Robin Hood vanished from them, while other characters including Maid Marian remained.

But Robin Hood survives in the Hal-an-Tow. This is a mystery play and pageant revived from an earlier celebration, thought to once have been widespread through Cornwall and rural areas elsewhere. It sets off early in the morning of Flora Day and makes its way around Helston. Its characters include Spanish sailors, St Piran, St George and the dragon, St Michael and the devil, and Robin Hood with his Merry Men. The song 'Hal-an-Tow' is sung and the verses acted out, all surrounded by a ring of people bedecked in greenery and spring flowers, determined to welcome the summer in raucous fashion.

A Traditional English Story for May

Jack-in-the-Green

Jack-in-the-Green is 9 feet tall, a dome of early summer foliage, beribboned and topped with a crown of flowers. On May Day in towns and cities throughout England he is woken from his slumber, and once awake he dances through the streets accompanied by chimney sweeps and by his attendants, the bogies: green-clad men and women who play music, dance around him and dab green on the noses of curious children. Once Jack has completed his procession, he is slain, to release the spirit of summer.

This strange tradition began in the 17th century in London, as a working-class celebration of trades and of a day off. Milk maids – who were probably continuing earlier Beltane traditions of the gathering at dawn of spring flowers, and the music and dancing – decorated their pails on May Day with silver cups, flowers and ribbons and then went from house to house wearing them on their heads and dancing for pennies.

May Day was also 'Chimney Sweeps' Day', and the sweeps started competing with the milk maids. The result was ever-bigger displays of foliage, flowers and silver to encourage tips, until the foliage covered them completely, and the tradition of Jack-in-the-Green was born.

This spread through the towns and cities of the south of England, but by the late 1800s it was strongly disapproved of and given almost entirely negative press, as its raucous, noisy, working-class fun clashed with Victorian sensibilities. It eventually died out in favour of more genteel May Day traditions.

The growing interest in Morris dancing in the 1970s and the Labour government's introduction of the May Day bank holiday combined to spark a revival, and Jack-in-the-Green is now seen in many towns and cities. The revival has morphed the tradition back into something more pagan and mystical, bringing at least a little of its original bawdiness, along with a celebration of the rebirth and renewal of early summer.

May's Full Moon

Mother's Moon | Bright Moon

In May the light of the full moon is reflected back
by reams of hawthorn hedges all blossoming white at
once. Hawthorn was for hundreds of years the farmers'
hedge of choice, and was used to create stock-proof
(and people-proof) enclosures, and so the English
countryside in particular is alight with sprays of pure
white blossom this month. Some Algonquian tribes
of North America call May's moon the Flower Moon,
and this is certainly a time of floral abundance in the
countryside and gardens. It is a fertile time and a time
for making babies – the medieval name for May's full
moon was Mother's Moon, which may refer to the
goddess Maia after whom May is named and who was
associated with midwives, motherhood and nursing.

A Song for May's Full Moon

'Drink Down the Moon'

Traditional, arr. Richard Barnard

There are several alternative titles for this folk song, including 'The Bird in the Bush' and 'Three Maids A-Milking Did Go', and all are euphemistic in the extreme. The three maids very straightforwardly invite their male friend into the woods with them, without worrying about what anyone else might think ('Let the people say little or say much'). Here the moon, and particularly the idea of 'drinking down the moon', is a shorthand for surrendering to sensuality and passion.

Three maidens a-milking did go
Three maidens a-milking did go
Oh, the wind it did blow high and the wind it did blow low
And it tossed their petticoats to and fro.

They met with a young man they did know
They met with a young man they did know
And they boldly asked of him if he had any skill
To catch them a small bird or two.

'Oh yes, I've a very fine skill
Oh yes, I've a very fine skill
Won't you come along with me to the yonder flowering tree
And I'll catch you a small bird or two.'

So off to the green woods went they
So off to the green woods went they
And he tapped at the bush and the bird it did fly in
A little above her lily-white knee.

And her sparkling eyes they did turn round
Just as if she was all in a swound
And she cried 'I have a bird, and a very pretty bird
and he's pecking away at his own ground.'

Here's a health to the bird in the bush
Here's a health to the bird in the bush
And we'll drink up the sun, and we'll drink down the moon
Let the people say little or say much.

Robin Hood and the Potter

This story was often acted out during the May Games, which traditionally consisted of the election of a May king and queen; a procession when the Hal-an-Tow song was performed; a Morris dance and a hobby horse dance; and a Robin Hood play. The story is typical of tales of Robin Hood, courting trouble with authority, generous to a fault and popular with the ladies.

One day in early summer, when the leaves were springing and there were blossoms on every bough, Robin Hood and his Merry Men saw a potter with a cart of pots coming through the forest. Little John, Robin's right-hand man, had met the man before in a fight, and he bet Robin that he would never be able to take a payment from him for passing by. Robin challenged the man and the two fought, the potter squarely beating Robin. Admitting defeat, Robin said, 'Let's have a little fun. You give me your clothes and I will give you mine, and I will go as you to Nottingham and sell your pots.' The potter agreed, and Little John warned Robin to avoid the Sheriff of Nottingham, who was a great enemy.

When he arrived in Nottingham, Robin – disguised as the potter – set up his stall and started crying, 'Pots! Great bargains!' and all of the women gathered around, whispering that he must be very new to making pots, to sell them so cheaply. When nearly all the pots were sold, Robin sent the last five to the wife of the Sheriff of Nottingham, who came to thank him and – taking a liking to him – invited him to dine with her and her husband. As they ate, two of the Sheriff's men talked of an upcoming shooting match, and Robin asked to join in. He easily beat the men, astonishing the Sheriff, so Robin told him that he had learned his skills shooting 100 bouts with Robin Hood, and that he would lead the Sheriff to him if he wished. Delighted, the Sheriff promised to reward him handsomely once Robin was captured.

When they were deep in the woods, Robin said, 'By my horn we shall find out if Robin Hood is nearby', and he blew a great blast. Soon the Merry Men arrived and robbed the Sheriff of his horse and the reward, sending him home by foot. 'If it weren't for the love of your dear wife,' said Robin, 'you would see much more trouble. The woman is very good.' And he told the Sheriff that he would be sending her a gift of a palfrey, a small, delicate horse popular among noblewomen. When the Sheriff finally got home and told his wife the tale, she laughed at him and said that at least now he had paid for the pots.

Robin returned to the greenwood tree, paid the potter ten pounds to cover the price of the pots, and told him that he was welcome to pass through the forest at any time.

June

The Naming of June

Ògmhios (Scots Gaelic) | *Juin* (Scots/Ulster Scots)
Meitheamh (Irish Gaelic) | *Mean-souree* (Manx)
Mehefin (Welsh) | *Metheven* (Cornish) | *Juîn* (Jèrriais)
Lilaieskero (Romani)

Several of the words used around the British Isles for June
are based on the root *haf*, meaning summer: the *hefin* of
Welsh Mehefin, the *heven* of Cornish Metheven and the
theamh of Irish Gaelic Meitheamh. The *me* prefix arises
from 'mean' or 'middle', as in the Manx Mean-souree,
which means 'middle summer'.

Scots, Ulster Scots and Jersey Jèrriais have derivations
of June, from the Latin name for the month, *Junius*, which
may be named after either the Roman goddess of marriage,
Juno, or the Latin *iuniores*, meaning 'younger ones', or
'juniors'. This could be a counterpoint to May's *maiores*,
meaning 'elders'. In keeping with this, the Scots Gaelic
Ògmhios means 'young month'.

Summer is here and the weather is suddenly gentle and
easy. Appropriately, the Romani name for June means 'month
of the summer'. In June many Romani families would have
taken (and still do take) time out to visit the largest horse
fair of the year, Appleby Fair, to dress up in their best, trade
horses and meet friends and relations. But there was also
work to be done. The Romani would undertake the seasonal
jobs that needed a large workforce for a short amount
of time.

Lilai appears in lots of 'summer' words, such as *lilaieski
rat* meaning 'Midsummer's Eve'and *lilaiesko cheriklo*
meaning 'swallow'.

Pilgrimage of the Month

Appleby Horse Fair

In the first week of June, the small town of Appleby in Cumbria fills with horses. Outside every shop, hotel and bar, horses are tethered. They splash in the river and trot along the lanes. Appleby Horse Fair holds a special importance in the British and Irish calendar, albeit one of which the vast majority of us are unaware. It is the largest event in the Gypsy, Romani and Traveller year, drawing around ten thousand members of the travelling community – British Romanichal, Irish Travellers, Scottish Gypsies and Travellers, and Kale (Welsh Romanies) from across Britain and Ireland, bringing with them a thousand caravans and several hundred horse-drawn carriages. The Appleby Horse Fair is the largest horse fair in the world and the biggest traditional Gypsy fair in Europe.

Since the late 18th century, it has been held just outside the town on what was once called Gallows Hill and is now called Fair Hill.

The main event is the washing of horses in the Sands, an area of shallows in the River Eden near Appleby town centre, after which they are 'flashed', or raced up and down nearby Long Marton Road, known among the Gypsies as Flashing Lane. The event lasts from the first Thursday in June to the following Tuesday (visitors are encouraged over the weekend), during which time palms are read and fortunes told, music played and horses traded. Travellers' wares are bought and sold, including Waterford crystal, gold earrings and chains, fine clothing and harnesses and carts. But above all this is a social gathering, particularly for the young men and women, for whom marrying within the community is traditional. Many future marriages will be set into motion. The fair shores up traditions, and acts as a reminder of the importance of their history, and the strength of their community for this small, scattered and still much persecuted minority.

Charm of the Month

Midsummer Cushions

In medieval times, 'Midsummer' was a loose community celebration that ran between St John the Baptist's Eve on 23rd June to St Peter's Day on 29th June. (You will note that actual Midsummer's Day is missed out completely, as 24th June, the Feast of St John the Baptist, was traditionally considered Midsummer.) The festivities centred around fires, flowers and feasting. Doors were hung with birch, fennel, lilies and wild flowers, and in the evenings bonfires and lamps would be lit outside shops and houses, food and drink laid out on tables, and neighbours invited to partake.

Midsummer cushions were the children's contribution to the floral bounty of what must have been a magical time. They were made in various ways – some from a board smeared with clay or mud and then stuck all over with petals, and some made from an actual cushion that was threaded with wild flowers. The Northamptonshire poet John Clare reported that children would take a piece of 'greensward', or turf, and stick it with meadow flowers to place in their cottages in a celebration of the natural abundance of this golden moment in the year. He entitled one of his books of poetry *The Midsummer Cushion*, and the custom has been revived in his native village of Helpston, where local children make Midsummer cushions to decorate his grave on the weekend closest to his birthday on 13th July.

June's Full Moon

Rose Moon | Dyad Moon

The medieval name for this month's moon is Rose Moon, reflecting the dog roses that are scrambling over hedgerows, their simple, pale pink petals catching the moonlight, as well as the abundance of roses wafting fragrantly from midnight gardens. It was also known as the Dyad Moon, 'dyad' meaning 'pair', and perhaps this is in reference to June being named after the Roman goddess of marriage, Juno, and being a month thought particularly favourable for weddings.

A Song for June's Full Moon

'Lament to the Moon'

Traditional, arr. Richard Barnard

As I went on my way at the close of the day a - bout the be-ginning of June, it was there in a glade that I saw a fair maid as she sang her la - ment to the moon: Roll a-long sil - very moon, guide the tra - veller's way while the night-ing - ale sings its sweet tune, but I'll ne - ver a-way with my true love to stray by the light of the sil - ve - ry moon.

This is an old Irish song that portrays the moon as comforting the broken-hearted, or at least illuminating them romantically. There may be roses and nightingales and a perfect silvery moon, but none of this will bring back a long-lost lover.

As I went on my way at the close of the day
About the beginning of June.
It was there in a glade that I saw a fair maid
As she sang her lament to the moon.

Roll along silvery moon, guide the traveller's way
While the nightingale sings its sweet tune.
But I'll never away with my true love to stray
By the light of the silvery moon.

My lover was brave as the hart on the hill
His arms they were brawny and strong.
So kind, so sincere, and he loved me so dear
As he sang me his old shanty songs.

But now he is gone, never more to return
Cut down like a rose in full bloom.
As he silently sleeps I am left here to weep
By the light of the silvery moon.

A Song for a Rose

'Rose in June'

Traditional

This pretty song was collected by Bob Copper, a member of the Copper Family – folk singers who passed songs down through the generations. Bob also acted as a collector and recorded this from George Fosbury in Hampshire in 1954. It is a song of love, petals and of wandering and picking in Midsummer.

Was down in the val - ley, the val - ley so deep to

pick some fine ros-es to keep my love sweet so let it be ear - ly late

or noon I'll en - joy my rose in June.

The violets make the meadows smell sweet,
But none with my roses can compete.

Chorus:
So let it be early, late or noon,
I'll enjoy my rose in June.

The rose in June's not half so sweet
As kisses where true lovers meet.

Chorus

Then I will drive my flock to the fold,
Let the weather blow warm or cold.

Chorus

Then I'll cut down the sweet myrtle tree,
To make a fine bower for Sally and me.

Chorus

Of every sweet flower that grows,
None can compare to my blooming rose.

Chorus

Dressing Up in June

Summer Solstice
at Stonehenge

The summer solstice falls between 20th and 21st June, when thousands of people gather at Stonehenge to watch the sun rising just to the left of the Heel Stone. (It is thought that there was once a second stone, and the sun would have been framed between it and the Heel Stone.) The historical basis for this is a little hazy. The exact ways in which people from the late Neolithic onwards made use of Stonehenge are fiercely debated, but it seems to have always been a place of gathering and ritual, and we know that those gatherings were centred around the solstices and the equinoxes. Stonehenge works as a great stone almanac of the year, the sun falling through particular slots between stones on the key dates.

Although it seems likely that the winter solstice saw the largest gatherings in ancient times, it is the summer solstice that now draws the greatest crowd, with up to ten thousand attendees. The only formalised dress for the event is the long white robe, the attire of the modern-day druids, for whom this is a religious occasion. Their ceremony is joyful and full of music and poetry, and includes – of course – a mock fight between the Holly King and the Oak King.

But the wider event is also host to a great creative flowering of interpretations of British folklore and mythology. Folkloric, pagan and mythical figures from around the year appear – the Green Man, the Mari Lwyd (a Welsh traditional folk costume made from a horse's skull), Maid Marian, Merlin, King Arthur, pagan goddesses, witches and wizards, horned men, unicorns, Morris dancers and the Nordic sun goddess Sunna. It is a great mash-up of anything and everything that may or may not reside in Britain's pagan past, with a few Aztecs and Native Americans thrown in for good measure. Perhaps the latter reflects a longing for the connection with the land and nature that is associated with indigenous cultures, and which many seek in Britain's lost paganism. Summer solstice at Stonehenge has become a great gathering of those who want to celebrate the turning of the seasons, and who wish to celebrate our pagan past, mysterious as it may be.

Folk Story of the Month

Merlin and the Making of Stonehenge

For hundreds of years – even as late as the 18th century – the folk belief about the construction of Stonehenge was based on that put forward by Geoffrey of Monmouth (c.1100–c.1155) in his chronicle *The History of the Kings of Britain* (c.1136). This is how the story goes.

To commemorate the hundreds of Britons treacherously slaughtered on Salisbury Plain during a supposed truce with the Saxons, King Aurelius Conanus decided to build a great monument. He set his carpenters and stonemasons to the task but they failed to come up with a plan grand or impressive enough, and so he sent for Merlin. Merlin said, 'If you want to grace the burial place of these men with a suitable monument, send for the Giant's Ring which is on Mount Killaraus in Ireland. There you will find a stone construction that no man of this age could erect unless he combined great skill and artistry. The stones are enormous and no man alive could move them. If they are placed in the same way around this site, then they will stand for ever.' The stones at Mount Killaraus had been placed there by two giants who had stolen them from Africa for their healing qualities, and would pour water over them and then use it to fill baths and heal the sick.

Merlin, together with the king's brother, Uther Pendragon, and 15,000 men, readied ships and set off for Ireland. There they battled and vanquished Irish forces and set about the stones. But the stones, being so vast, proved impossible to move, so Merlin used his magic to move them to the ships. Once they had been transported to Salisbury Plain, Aurelius ordered Merlin to erect the stones in the same pattern in which they had been arranged in Ireland, and he did so, and Stonehenge was created. After their deaths, Uther Pendragon and Aurelius were buried within the ring of stones.

Folk Song of the Month

'Midsummer Carol (Lemady)'

Traditional, arr. Richard Barnard

This traditional West Country ballad makes reference to
Midsummer wooing. On Midsummer's morning young
men would get up at dawn to gather posies of flowers and
present them to the object of their affections, a practice
known as 'lemady'.

A midsummer morning as I was a-walking
The fields and the meadows were green and gay,
The birds sang so sweetly, so sweet and adoring
So early in the morning at break of day.
The birds sang so sweetly ...

It's hark, O hark to the nightingale singing,
The lark she is taking her flight in the air,
The turtle doves now in the green bough are building,
The sun is just a-glimm'ring, arise my fair.
The turtle doves now ...

Arise and arise, go and gather a posy,
The sweetest of flowers that grow in yonder grove.
O, I'll pick them all, lilies, pinks and roses;
It's all for my Lemady, the girl I love.
O, I'll pick them all ...

O, Lemady! O, Lemady! The sweetest of flowers,
The sweetest of flowers my eyes did ever see
And I'll play a tune on the pipes of ivory
So early in the morning at break of day.
And I'll play a tune ...

A Sea Shanty for June

'Blow Ye Winds'

An unusually mystical subject for a sea shanty – most are concerned with far more practical and earthy subjects such as money, women and work – but to be fair it does approach mermaids and mermen in a characteristically robust fashion. 'Blow Ye Winds' is a capstan shanty, used for hauling up the anchor.

As I walked out one mor-ning fair all in the month of June, I
ov-er-heard an Ir-ish girl a-sing-ing this old tune, sing-ing,
Blow ye winds in the mor-ning, blow ye winds, high-ho!
See all clear your run-ning gear, and blow, boys, blow!

Our ship she lay at anchor with the men at work about
When 'neath the bow we heard a splash and then a lusty shout.
Singing, Blow ye winds in the morning,
Blow ye winds, high-ho!
See all clear your running gear,
And blow, boys, blow!

'Man overboard!' The lookout cried and forward we all ran,
There hanging to our larboard chains we saw a green merman.
Singing, Blow ye winds...

His hair was blue and eyes were green, his mouth as big as three,
The long green tail he sat on was still waving in the sea.
Singing, Blow ye winds...

He spoke to us as bold as brass 'A plea I have to bring:
You've dropped your anchor on my house
and trapped my family in.'
Singing, Blow ye winds...

Our anchor we brought up at once and set his family free,
We asked him how he came to be a creature in the sea.
Singing, Blow ye winds...

He told us he fell overboard while sailing in a gale
And down below where seaweeds grow, he met a girl with a tail.
Singing, Blow ye winds...

She saved his life, became his wife, and his legs changed instantly
And now he lives in comfort at the bottom of the sea.
Singing, Blow ye winds...

July

The Naming of July

Iuchar (Scots Gaelic) | *Julie* (Scots/Ulster Scots)
Iúil (Irish Gaelic) | *Jerry-souree* (Manx)
Gorffennaf (Welsh) | *Gortheren* (Cornish)
Juilet (Jèrriais) | *Kasekero* (Romani)

Julius Caesar named July 'Julius' after himself in 46 BC, as a pat on the back for reforming the Roman calendar and creating the (you guessed it) Julian calendar. Before this, July was known as *Quintilis*, the fifth month (the first month then being March), but no trace of *Quintilis* has remained in the names of the month, while several are based on Julius. The Manx Jerry-souree may look as if it is related but, in fact, *jerry* means 'end' and *souree* means 'summer'. This seems impossibly pessimistic to our modern way of thinking but is related to a more complex understanding of the agricultural patterns of the year than to any more romantic sense of summer (or indeed to the temperature). Summer was considered the months of growth – May, June and July – and August was when crops switched their energies to fruiting and ripening, and the time for the first harvests. Hence July was seen as the last month of summer. Similarly, the Welsh Gorffennaf is from *gorfen* meaning 'end' and *haf* meaning 'summer'. The Scots Gaelic Iuchar and the Irish Gaelic Iúil have another root entirely – they are thought to be related to *fiuch*, meaning 'to boil or seethe', presumably relating to those sweltering Outer Hebrides summers.

From high summer through to autumn, all of the Romani names of the month refer to the big seasonal jobs that the Romani would have traditionally returned to year after year. July's Kaseskero – month of the hay – is the first of these and refers to haymaking. Farmers then, as now, grew fields of grasses and wild flowers and then turned them into dried hay to store, so that they would have a source of such stuff to feed their livestock over winter.

Charm of the Month

Bees

Though you can't pop a bee into your pocket to cling to in times of worry (ouch), they have traditionally had so many lucky associations that they can surely count as charms, albeit living, breathing, honey-making ones. A bee landing on you is very lucky, and one flying into your house will bring luck or a visitor, as long as you let it find its own way out naturally. Their lucky symbolism must be connected to their great importance in creating such a vital and delicious source of food. There are also several superstitions relating to their sensitive nature and the perils of treating them badly, presumably stemming from their propensity to fly away or die if they don't find conditions exactly to their liking. Bees will not stay in an argumentative household, and they particularly object to swearing. A hive should never be owned by one person; indeed, it is at its luckiest when owned by an unmarried man and an unmarried woman. And the hive needs to be kept informed – if a daughter of the household is to be married, you must whisper it to the bees. You must also do this when a member of the household dies, as the bees must be allowed to mourn or they will fly away. Needless to say, to kill a bee will bring terrible luck.

honey bee

A Cornish Folk Tale for July

The Curse of the Doom Bar

The second Sunday in July is Sea Sunday. This is the day
the Catholic Church offers services and blessings for
seafarers and their families, and raises funds for the
Apostleship of the Sea, often known as Stella Maris,
which offers ministry and support for sailors in ports.
Stella Maris, or Star of the Sea, is another name for the
Virgin Mary, who is believed to be the guide and protector
of seafarers – though possibly not those who go about
shooting mermaids.

There was once a time, many years ago, when Padstow was
a deep and wide natural harbour, blessed with the protection
of a beautiful mermaid, or merry maid, as they are called
in Cornwall. Large boats sailed in and out freely, and the
harbour and town were prosperous and busy. But as any
sailor knows, mermaids are not to be trifled with, and these
blissful years were not to last. One day the mermaid was
sitting on the rocks at Hawker's Cove combing her long
golden hair, when she noticed a young man walking among
the rocks, holding a gun. He was a local man, a sailor called
Tristram Bird, and was out hunting seals. The mermaid was
unhappy to see this and decided to distract him in order to
save her seal friends, and so to catch his attention she started
singing the most beautiful song. Tristram forgot his hunting
and fell instantly in love with her, and he ran to her begging
for her hand in marriage. But she laughed and rejected him,
telling him that she only wished to stop him from shooting
the seals. At this he flew into a rage and shot her instead!
With her dying breath she cursed the harbour with a 'bar of
doom', and picked up a handful of sand, flinging it from
Hawker's Cove to Trebetherick Bay. That night a storm blew
up and by morning a sand bar lay across the bay, strewn with
wrecked boats and the bodies of sailors.

A Sailor's Song

'The Mermaid'

Traditional

'The Mermaid' is one of the 'Child Ballads' (number 289) collected by folklorist Francis James Child in England and Scotland in the second half of the 19th century. It is a sea ballad – sung by sailors during resting times – rather than a sea shanty, or working song. As is often the case in folklore, the sighting of the mermaid is a sign of impending disaster.

'Twas a Fri-da-y morn when we set sail, Our ship not far from the land, When we did es spy a fair mer-maid, With a comb and a glass in her hand, her hand, her hand. With a comb and a glass in her hand. Oh the o-cean waves do roll, And the stor-my winds do blow, And as we jol-ly sai-lor boys were up, were up a-loft, And the land lub-bers ly-ing down be-low, be-low, be-low And the land lub-bers ly-ing down be-low.

Up spoke the captain of our gallant ship
And a brave old skipper was he
'This fishy mermaid has warned me of our doom
We shall sink to the bottom of the sea, the sea, the sea
We shall sink to the bottom of the sea.'

Chorus:
Oh the ocean waves do roll
And the stormy winds do blow
And as we jolly sailor boys were up, were up aloft
And the landlubbers lying down below, below, below
And the landlubbers lying down below.

Up spoke the first mate of our gallant ship
And a well-spoken man was he
'I have me a wife in Salem by the sea
And tonight she a widow will be, will be, will be
And tonight she a widow will be.'

Chorus

Then up spoke the cabinboy, of our gallant ship
And a fair-haired lad was he
'I'm not quite sure I can spell mermaid
But I'm going to the bottom of the sea, the sea, the sea
But I'm going to the bottom of the sea.'

Chorus

Then three times around spun our gallant ship
And three times around spun she
Three times around spun our gallant ship
And she sank to the bottom of the sea, the sea, the sea
And she sank to the bottom of the sea.

Chorus

Folk Story of the Month

The Weardale Fairies

A key element in this story of fairy folk is the glow-worm, a beetle famous for the greenish-orange light that the females emit at night – but only in June–July.

A young farmer's daughter who lived in Stanhope, in Weardale in the Pennines, was out gathering wild flowers when she heard beautiful music, played on the pipe, fiddle and drum. Beguiled, she followed the sound to a cleft between two rocks, and looking through the crack she could see fairy folk dancing by candlelight. She knew it wasn't safe to linger, so she tore herself away to run home.

Her parents were horrified when she told them. 'Oh, my love, we have as good as lost you!' cried the mother. 'The fairy folk hate to be spied upon and they will come and fetch you tonight.' They put every possible protection in place, but in the morning the girl was gone. The distraught father set off for the local wise woman's house and begged her to tell him how to win his daughter back. 'You must take the fairies three gifts,' said the woman. 'A light that does not burn; a part of an animal gained without shedding blood; and a live chicken without a bone in its body.' The farmer thanked her, but set off full of despair.

Along the road he was roused from his troubles by a scrawny beggar, and he dropped the poor man a coin. The beggar said, 'I have little to give you in return, but take this glow-worm I use to light my way at night.' The farmer was astonished and accepted the glow-worm with great thanks. Walking further, he noticed a lizard struggling in a twist of wire and so he bent down to free it, but as he did so the lizard's tail came away in his hand and the lizard scuttled away, unharmed. Feeling happier by the moment, the farmer continued along the road. Soon he heard a great struggle in the bushes and saw a thrush being attacked by a hawk.

He threw a stone and hit the hawk, and as the thrush flew away, it sang, 'An egg under a hen! An egg under a hen!' The farmer rushed home and, taking a warm egg from under his broody hen, he set off for the fairies' lair. When he heard the music, he looked through the cleft in the rocks and spied his daughter, pale and exhausted, dancing with the fairy folk.

'I bring you three gifts in exchange for my daughter!' he shouted, and he pushed the gifts through the gap. In a moment there was a great crash and a flash of light, then all fell silent and dark in the rock. The farmer's heart sank, but then from behind him came a voice crying, 'Father!' – and there was his daughter, laughing and smiling and ready to return safely home...and to never, ever spy on the fairy folk again.

A Sea Shanty for July

'Santiana'

A song for St Anne's feast day, on 26th July. There is confusion about the origins and meaning of this shanty, which may have had an African American tune at its birth. It could be about the 19th-century Mexican general Santa Anna, in whose army many British sailors deserted their ships to fight, or it might be for St Anne, the patron saint of sailors and the protector from storms. Either way, it apparently made its way inland from US coastal ports and became as popular among cowboys as it was among sailors.

This is a pump shanty, used when pumping water out of the hulls of leaky wooden ships, a frequent and exhausting job much improved by the singing of a shanty.

I wish I was old Stor-my's son Hoo-ray San-ti-a-na! I'd build a ship of a thou-sand ton Heave a-way to the plains of Me-xi-co!

I'd give her whisky an' lots o' gin
Hooray Santiana!
And stay in the port where she was in
Heave away to the plains of Mexico!

Though times are hard an' wages low
Hooray Santiana!
'Tis time for us to roll an' go
Heave away to the plains of Mexico!

Oh, Mexico, where the land lies low
Hooray Santiana!
Oh, Mexico, where the wind don't blow
Heave away to the plains of Mexico!

Dressing Up in July

Rose Queens

A number of villages around the UK will see the crowning of their Rose Queen this month. Rose Queen coronations arose mainly in areas where there was a stronger tradition of 'Wakes Week' than of May Day celebrations. Wakes Week was the name adopted by factory owners for the weeks (and later fortnights) when they would shut their factories down and give the whole workforce their holiday at once, as a more economical alternative to staggered holidays. Local festivals and fêtes in the newly industrialised towns of the Midlands and the North of England, especially the Northwest, often took on the name 'wakes'. The organisers of these wakes may have simply fancied a May Queen-like tradition, but the wakes fell in the summer rather than the spring and so Rose Queens were created. They are essentially May Queens – teenage girls or young women dressed in white and garlanded with flowers – but with roses rather than lily of the valley and bluebells in their hair.

Several of these traditions appear to have been started, or revived, by the would-be Rose Queens themselves. For example, the first Rose Queen coronation in the village of Wrea Green in Lancashire occurred in July 1924 when a group of seven local girls who had watched a Rose Queen procession in a nearby village decided that they should have one of their own. They chose a queen and attendants and made a rose crown, then set off around the village green, but only got part way round before losing their nerve and retreating to a local garden for the coronation. Since then there have been over 100 Rose Queens in the village, and the coronation has become a central part of Wrea Green's Field Day festivities.

Although Rose Queen festivals are much less common now than they were a century ago, they can still be found at villages around the country.

July's Full Moon

Wyrt Moon | Mead Moon

July is lush and green. *Wyrt* is an Old English word for 'herbs', and the medieval name Wyrt Moon for July's full moon reflects the fact that while little has ripened yet, greenery and herbs are plentiful. This is also the time beekeepers take their first honey of the year, and so the making of mead – a fermented honey drink – could begin, an important pastime in medieval Britain.

A Song for July's Full Moon

'The Man in the Moon'

Traditional, arr. Richard Barnard

This jaunty old Sussex dance tune takes as its subject the poor man in the moon himself, who, for all his grandeur and beauty, must get a bit lonesome up there on his own.

The man in the moon seems to lead a queer life
With no one around him, not even a wife;
No friends to console him, no children to kiss,
No chance of his joining a party like this.
He changes his lodgings each quarter anew
After leaving a circus, a crescent will do
If he rents in these quarters so fast going by
I imagine his rent is uncommonly high,
But he's used to the high life, all circles agree,
For none move in circles as high up as he.
Though nobles go up in their royal balloon,
They can't get to meet him, the man in the moon.

It is said that some people are moonstruck, we find,
And the man in the moon could be out of his mind.
But it can't be for love, for he's quite on his own,

No lovers to meet him by moonlight alone...
It can't be ambition, for rivals he's none,
At least he is only eclipsed by the sun,
But when drinking, I say, he is seldom surpassed,
For he always looks best when he's seen through a glass.
Oh, the man in the moon a new light on us throws,
He's a man we all talk of but nobody knows.
And though a high subject, I'm getting in tune,
I'll just sing a song for the man in the moon.

♩ = 152

When a bum-per is filled it is ve-xing no doubt to__ find when you rise that the

wine has run out, And it's sure - ly an e - qua-lly un-plea-sant thing to be

asked for a song when you've no-thing to sing. I could try some-thing old if an

old one would do, but the world it is cra-ving to hear some-thing new. What

do I se - lect for the words or the tune? I, in fact, know no more than 'The

Man in the Moon'. Oh, the Man in the Moon a new light on us throws. He's a

man we all talk of but no - bo - dy knows, and__ though a high sub-ject, I'm

ge-tting in tune, I'll__ just sing a song for the Man in the Moon.

August

The Naming of August

Lùnastal (Scots Gaelic) | *August* (Scots/Ulster Scots)
Lúnasa (Irish Gaelic) | *Luanistyn* (Manx)
Awst (Welsh) | *Est* (Cornish) | *Août* (Jèrriais)
Giveskero (Romani)

After Julius Caesar started the Julian calendar reform and rewarded himself with a month (July), along came Augustus Caesar to complete the job, and so he gave himself a month, too, hence August. Most of the languages of the British Isles have variants on this as their names for August (including the very French Août in Jèrriais). However, Scots Gaelic, Irish Gaelic and Manx all name the month after the Gaelic festival of Lughnasadh, one of the four Gaelic agricultural markers of the year (along with Imbolc, Beltane and Samhain). Lughnasadh is the first harvest festival of the year and particularly celebrates the first cuts of wheat and the first fruits: nature has shifted from growth to ripening.

In the Romani year August was the month of the corn, which means that it is time for the wheat to be brought in (corn having always been used as a generic term for cereal, rather than meaning sweetcorn). The wheat harvest has long been the biggest event in the rural year. Whole rural families would move from farm to farm around their village to help harvest the wheat, and there are a great number of traditions associated with it. This is particularly the case at the end of the harvest, when a corn dolly would be made from the last sheaf cut and would keep the 'spirit of the corn' or the 'corn mother' safe throughout the winter; the following spring, the corn dolly would be buried in the field as it was ploughed and sown.

A Song for Harvest

'John Barleycorn'

Traditional

This apparently macabre song is really a celebration of John Barleycorn, the personification of the barley crop. Despite his terrible treatment at the hands of the men who see to him – throwing clods upon his head, cutting him at the knee, grinding him between stones – none of them can do without him, and he proves the strongest of them all, presumably seeing them off in the form of beer and whisky.

There were three men came out o' the west, their for-tunes for to try, And these three men made a sol-emn vow John Bar-ley-corn must die, They ploughed, and sowed, and harrowed him in, threw clods up on his head, And these three men made a sol-emn vow John Barley-corn was dead.

They let him lie for a very long time
Till the rains from heaven did fall
And little Sir John sprung up his head
And so amazed them all.

They let him stand for a long time,
Till he looked both pale and wan,
And little Sir John grew a long, long beard
And so become a man.

They hired men with the scythes so sharp
To cut him off at the knee;
They rolled him and tied him by the waist –
Serving him most barbarously.

They hired men with their crab-tree sticks
To cut him skin from bone
And the miller he served him worse than that
For he ground him between two stones.

Here's little Sir John in the nut brown bowl
And brandy in the glass
And little Sir John in the nut brown bowl
Proved the strongest man at last.

The huntsman he can't hunt the fox
Nor so loudly to blow his horn
And the tinker he can't mend kettle nor pots
Without little Lord Barleycorn.

August's Full Moon

Grain Moon | Lynx Moon

Spend time in the countryside this month and it is easy to see why the name Grain Moon was once used for August's full moon. This is the moment that fields of wheat are ripening to soft gold, with warm breezes rippling them in the moonlight. Harvest time has begun. The name Lynx Moon has not stood the test of time in the same way, namely because lynxes were driven out of Britain 1,300 years ago. It is a bit of a mystery as to why lynxes might have been so noticeable this month to warrant calling the moon after them – however, they do hunt at night, and August might have been a time when there were more of them around, as the cubs born in spring grew large enough to hunt. A more likely explanation might be that the word lynx is derived from the Middle English word *leuk*, meaning 'light', or 'brightness', given to lynxes because of their pale yellow, reflective eyes. 'Lynx' might therefore have been a reference to the brightness of the moon itself (perhaps as a result of the 'moon illusion', which is often more noticeable in late summer) rather than because of the presence of this very shy animal.

A Song for August's Full Moon

'Moon Shine Tonight'

Traditional, arr. Richard Barnard

A Jamaican folk song from a time when there was no electricity to illuminate night-time gatherings, and it made sense to time parties for the full moon, and then dance and sing in its light.

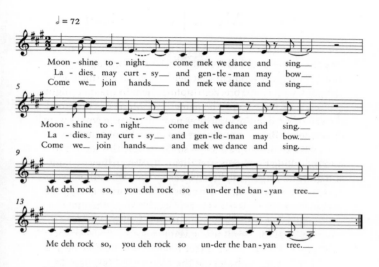

Moon shine tonight come mek we dance and sing.
Moon shine tonight come mek we dance and sing.

Chorus:
Me deh rock so
You de rock so
Under the banyan tree.
Me deh rock so
You deh rock so
Under the banyan tree.

Ladies may curtsy and gentleman may bow.
Ladies may curtsy and gentleman may bow.

Chorus

Come we join hands and mek we dance and sing.
Come we join hands and mek we dance and sing.

Charm of the Month

White Heather

In August the ling heather is coming into full bloom
across Scotland's moorlands and glens, turning them
beautiful shades of purple. Among this purple sea you
might find a rare patch of white heather, which is
considered a lucky charm and historically sold at fairs
and tucked into bride's bouquets. There are various
stories as to why it is lucky, but the root of it might be
its rarity – it is thought to be a sport (spontaneous
mutation) of purple heather. It was adopted by the clan
called Clanranald whose members wore it into battle
and won a miraculous victory, and by Clan Macpherson
because of the story that a member of the clan fell asleep
on a patch after the Battle of Culloden and was missed
by an English search party. There seems a good chance
that Queen Victoria, with her love of all things Scottish,
took the germ of a story and turned it into a full-blown
craze, as the earliest confirmed mention of the superstition
is found in her hugely popular book *Leaves from the Journal
of Our Life in the Highlands from 1848 to 1861*. Nevertheless,
it has since been conferring luck on brides and on anyone
who manages to track down an elusive sprig.

Pilgrimage of the Month

Pilgrims' Way, Lindisfarne, for the Feast of St Aidan

Stretching out across Beal Sands on the Northumberland coast is a line of poles 3.5m high, set into the sand. They follow a route trodden by saints and pilgrims for at least 1,500 years, 5km across the mudflats towards Lindisfarne, or Holy Island. This is a tidal pilgrimage, washed over by the sea and visited by seals twice a day, and you must time your visit carefully if you wish to walk, setting out on the falling tide. Summer is a good bet, as it is warm enough to walk barefoot, which is the recommended way: in places the mud can be up to 30cm deep so if you insist on footwear you will either ruin your walking boots or lose your wellies.

31st August is the feast day of St Aidan, the Apostle of Northumbria. Aidan, who was of Irish descent, was a monk brought from the Isle of Iona by Oswald, King of Northumbria, who tasked Aidan with restoring Christianity to the Anglo-Saxons. The religion had been brought to Britain by the Romans, but by 634, on this northeast coast of England, it had been largely displaced by Anglo-Saxon paganism. Aidan founded a priory on Lindisfarne and travelled extensively through Northumbria, spreading the gospel among aristocracy and the poor alike. The site of the original priory is now a church, rebuilt by the Normans, and the oldest structure on the island – its remains can be visited.

The origin of the name Lindisfarne is uncertain but 'lindis' may refer to the people of the Kingdom of Lindsey, which is part of modern Lincolnshire, and 'farne' may come from Old English *fearena*, which means 'traveller', underlining Lindisfarne's position as an ancient place of pilgrimage. There are various long-distance pilgrimage routes that lead here, including St Oswald's Way, stretching from Hadrian's Wall, and St Cuthbert's Way, named after the second Bishop of Lindisfarne and stretching from Melrose in the Scottish borders. All end up on this otherworldly stretch of sand and mud, the wind whipping in from the North Sea and the cries of gulls in the air.

A Sea Shanty for August

'The Oak and the Ash'

Shanties are far less seasonal than landlubber folk songs, perhaps because the weather in the Atlantic was either cold and wet or really cold and wet. However, in this West Country shanty we do hear that the oak, ash and elm trees are all in leaf and so we can safely assume that it is summer, at least in this homesick sailor's imagination. This is a fo'c's'cle, or forebitter, shanty, sung in the sailors' downtime, as such yearning songs often seem to have been.

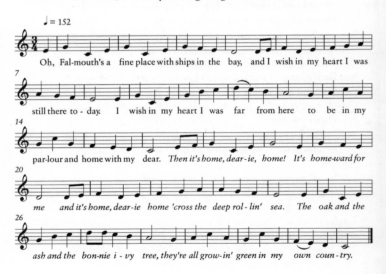

In Plymouth out walking a girl I did meet.
She carried a babe as she walked through the street,
And I thought of the young maid who once caught my eye,
When I left her some silver, a cradle to buy.

Then it's home, dearie, home! It's homeward for me
And it's home, dearie, home 'cross the deep rollin' sea.
The oak and the ash and the bonnie ivy tree,
They're all growin' green in my own country.

And if it's a girl she will stay here with me,
And if it's a boy he will plough the blue sea.
He'll plough the blue sea as his daddy had done
With his pea jacket blue like a true sailor's son.

Then it's home...

Moko Jumbies at Notting Hill Carnival

At the end of August, Moko Jumbies will stalk the streets of west London during the Notting Hill Carnival. These stilt-walkers are up to 4.5m tall, with painted faces and colourful costumes. They are a link back through the origins of Carnival in Trinidad to the folklore of the west coast of Africa, from where so many people were taken into slavery and transported to the Caribbean islands.

The Trinidadian Carnival began as a pre-Lent, Mardi Gras masquerade among French and Spanish settlers. Slave masters would black up and dress as field slaves, or *nègres de jardin*, and their wives would dress as the *mulâtresses*, the women of mixed racial origin who were the children of raped slaves. On the abolition of slavery in 1834 the Carnival became popular among the emancipated former slaves, and the tradition was turned on its head: comedy characters such as Dame Lorraine – a white woman with huge bosom and bottom – became regulars, and revellers wore white masks and stuffed clothes that mocked the plantation owners. Moko Jumbies became standard characters at around the same time: Moko is a West African god of retribution, and the word Jumbie, which was added later, means 'spirit'. Moko Jumbies are protective spirits, able to see trouble coming from their great height. In Trinidad they were thought to reside in the big old silk cotton trees on plantations where so many slaves were hanged.

The Windrush generation, West Indians who answered the call to emigrate to the UK to help reduce Britain's post-war labour shortages, found themselves in an often hostile land. In January 1959, the journalist Claudia Jones introduced Carnival arts and culture to London when she held an indoor carnival event to unite the community after the Notting Hill riots of August 1958. Then, in the summer of 1966, Rhaune Laslett started the Notting Hill Festival with children dressed in costume, joined by musicians. This was the birth of the carnival street parade, which now attracts over a million revellers. Some of the traditional costumes have died out, but the Moko Jumbies can still be seen, high above, watching over the festival-goers.

Folk Story of the Month

Gang Gang Sarah

A Story from Trinidad and Tobago

This story speaks of the longing for home felt among the slaves and of the impossibility of return to Africa, and even to their former idea of themselves, once they had arrived in the West Indies. Having tasted the salt of their adopted home, they were transformed, and there was no going back.

One stormy night a witch named Sarah was blown across the sea from Africa to Tobago, and landed quite neatly in the village of Les Coteaux. Her family had long before been transported there in slave ships, and Sarah had come to look for them in Golden Lane, near Les Coteaux, as she was desperate to take care of them. Although she didn't find them, she decided to stay and help the people out. She was wise and kind and she knew which herbs to give to the people for which ailments, and what potion a woman could use to make a man fall in love with her. She took care of the pregnant women and acted as midwife, which earned her the name 'Gang Gang Sarah', and she was even asked to name some of the children.

Sarah married a man called Tom, whom she had known as a child in Africa, and together they lived to a ripe old age. When Tom died, Sarah decided that it was time to fly home.

She climbed to the highest limbs of a silk cotton tree and jumped. But sadly she had lost her powers of flight, having tasted the salt of her new home, which, of course, no witch must do if they hope to keep their powers intact. She fell to the ground and died, and was buried next to Tom in the plantation cemetery, where their headstones can still be seen to this day.

The tree Gang Gang Sarah is said to have fallen from is the largest of its kind on Tobago, and for many years a sign alongside it read, 'This silk cotton tree was considered sacred by the African slaves who believed that the spirits of their ancestors lived in its branches.'

Folk Song of the Month

'Mangoes'

Traditional, arr. Richard Barnard

Calypso was the original music of the Notting Hill Carnival, and even now the climax of the UK calypso year is the Calypso Monarch Finals, always held on the Thursday before Carnival. The style is likely descended from West African Kaiso and Canboulay songs that were sung in the plantations as a method of communication when slaves were not allowed to speak to each other. It very literally arrived in Britain with the Windrush generation: when the HMT *Empire Windrush* first arrived at London's Tilbury Docks from the Caribbean on 21st June 1948, several well-known calypsonians were on board. A Pathé News camera filmed 'king of calypso' Lord Kitchener singing 'London Is the Place for Me' as he disembarked.

'Mangoes' is a Trinidadian folk song, sung to a calypso beat and with lyrics in a mixture of Creole, English and French, as reflects the island's heritage. No less than eight types of mango are listed in the two verses.

Mangoes, mangoes, mangoes!
Mango vert, mango teen,
Mango vert, mango teen,
I want a penny to buy
Mango vert, mango teen.
Give me a penny to buy
Mango vert, mango teen.
Mango doodou, sousay-matin
Savez-vous all for me
Mango doodou, sousay-matin
Savez-vous all for me.

Mangoes, mangoes, mangoes!
Mango rose, mango starch,
Mango rose, mango starch,
I want a penny to buy
Mango rose, mango starch.
Give me a penny to buy
Mango rose, mango starch.
Mango zapico, calabash
Savez-vous all for me
Mango zapico, calabash
Savez-vous all for me.

September

The Naming of September

Sultain (Scots Gaelic)
September (Scots/Ulster Scots)
Meán Fómhair (Irish Gaelic) | *Mean-fouyir* (Manx)
Medi (Welsh) | *Gwynngala* (Cornish)
Septembre (Jèrriais) | *Rigerimaskero* (Romani)

September was the Roman name for this month, which means 'seventh month', dating from the time when March was the start of the year. The English names for the months follow this pattern for the rest of the year, October being the eighth month, November the ninth and December the tenth. Most of the languages of the British Isles take a more agricultural approach to September. Meán Fómhair in Irish Gaelic means 'mid' and 'harvest', and is echoed in the Manx Mean-fouyir, while the Welsh Medi means 'harvest' or 'reaping'. As often, the Cornish name for the month – Gwynngala – arises from Breton rather than from any of the languages of the British Isles. In Breton, September is *Gwengolo*, which may come from *gwenn* meaning 'white', and *kolo* meaning 'straw', a reference to crops ripening and stems blanching in the sun. The Scots Gaelic Sultain is from a word that means 'pleasing, pleasant, fat': there are good times and feasting to be had as the harvest comes in.

This is such an abundant month that in the Romani language the name for the month is a reflection of this abundance, as it translates as month of the gathering, or of the harvests. Living so fully in the landscape, the Romanies have always made use of wild harvests, and this month, golden with late-summer sunshine and with just a hint of autumnal cool in the air, there would have been blackberries and elderberries glistening and hazelnuts turning toasty brown in the hedgerows by the side of the road.

Folk Story of the Month

Herne the Hunter

We are into deer-hunting season now, and so here is a tale of one of the greatest hunters ever known, turned vengeful spirit of the forest.

Herne was the head forester of Richard II in the 14th century, with dominion over the Windsor Castle royal forest and hunting park. His skills were immense: his arrow was true, he could anticipate every move the deer would make, and he was a great horseman, riding like a gale blowing through the ancient trees. He was also handsome, tall and sturdy like an oak, and the king favoured him greatly.

This made the other foresters jealous, and one moonless night they met in the forest to plot against him. As they gathered, a stranger appeared on a large black steed. They couldn't see his face, but in a deep voice he said, 'I will help to stop this man who has stolen the king's affections, and ask in return only that you each grant me one request when the deed is done.' Too cowardly to deal with Herne themselves, the men agreed, despite their foreboding.

The next day, when the king called the men together for the hunt, Herne was saddled up and ready to go. But as they set off, his horse reared and bucked and crashed into the king's steed. Throughout the hunt Herne lagged behind, never taking the lead, and when he was called upon to finish off a tired stag, he missed his mark. This continued over the weeks that followed: Herne had lost his skills, and the king dismissed him from his post. Heartbroken, Herne walked deep into the forest and hanged himself from an oak tree.

Soon rumours began of a terrifying woodland spirit seen in the forest. He looked like Herne, was as tall, broad and skilful as Herne, but had a great pair of antlers sprouting from his head. Now the foresters were scared, and soon the stranger appeared to them again.

He told them that when Herne appeared before them, they were to obey his every command, and that he would take the immortal soul of any that didn't. Almost immediately, Herne appeared. He made them meet him by the oak at midnight and then led them on a hunt through the night, only letting them crawl home to their beds as dawn broke. This he commanded night after night, until the men were so exhausted and useless that they confessed all to the king, who had them executed.

Herne's oak was blown down in 1863, but Queen Victoria had it replaced with a new oak on the same spot. That tree was removed in 1906 but yet another oak was planted in its place and today bears the title of Herne's Oak. Even now, those who live around the forest hear the sound of hunting horns at midnight, and some have even glimpsed a ghostly hunt chasing through the moonlit trees.

Charm of the Month

Corn Dollies

The corn spirit lives in the crop, and at harvest time it is made homeless, which can't be good.

The idea of the 'spirit of the corn' – corn being a generic name for grain crops such as wheat and barley – was prevalent in pre-Christian, pagan communities throughout Europe. It must have at its heart the vast importance of this crop to the communities that farmed it. Sometimes the corn spirit is male – see the well-known folk song 'John Barleycorn' for a manly personification – but the idea of the 'corn mother' and 'corn maiden' was strong, too. The harvest would have been carried out by gangs of men, women and children, and the cutting of the final sheaf of corn took on a great significance, representing the end of a period of extremely hard work, the beginning of the harvest feast, and the housing of the spirit of the corn itself. This final sheaf was held up and proclaimed, then taken away and woven or plaited into a dolly that became the centrepiece of the end-of-harvest celebrations. After this, the dolly would be safely housed to keep the spirit of the corn happy over the winter, and in the spring it was ploughed into the earth with the new crop's seeds.

Pilgrimage of the Month

St Michael's Way for Michaelmas

The most famous European pilgrimage is the Camino de Santiago, a network of paths leading to the Catedral de Santiago de Compostela, Spain. The Cathedral is one of only three in the world built over the tomb of an apostle of Jesus, in this case St James the Great. The Camino, consisting of a network of pilgrims' ways, has been a major pilgrimage route since medieval times and has seen a great revival over the past decades, with the Camino Francés, through France and Spain, the most popular route. This has led surrounding countries to investigate how their own pilgrims would have travelled there, and to reinstate their own pilgrim paths.

One of the pilgrim routes in the Camino de Santiago network is the St Michael's Way, running roughly 20km from the north Cornish coast at Lelant to the south Cornish coast at Marazion, overlooking St Michael's Mount. Archaeology and old shipping records suggest that pilgrims travelling from Ireland and Wales to complete the Camino took this land route to avoid sailing the perilous waters around Land's End. St Michael's Way is a beautiful route in itself, and September, the month of Michaelmas, is a fine month to walk it. It works its way along country lanes and bridleways to Trencrom Hill, the site of an ancient hill fort and from where you can take in a panoramic view of both coasts and down towards Land's End, looking ahead to St Michael's Mount surrounded by glittering seas, and the end point of this particular leg of pilgrimage.

The paths of St Michael's Way are now waymarked by St James's scallop shell, just as those of the rest of the Camino are. It is now an official extension of the Camino Inglés, which runs approximately 75km from A Coruña in northern Spain to Santiago de Compostela. Historical evidence suggests that this is where ships of pilgrims would arrive from England. As pilgrims must walk at least 100km to receive a certificate of pilgrimage, they can now do so along the Camino Inglés if they first journey coast to coast across this narrow and beautiful slice of Cornwall towards St Michael's Mount.

A Song for Michaelmas

'The Nutting Girl'

Traditional

Nuts were once an essential source of free food for poor rural families, and teenagers would be sent off into the woods during nutting season to gather what they could. With predictable results. Nutting became a byword for saucier pursuits, leading to the once-common phrase 'a good year for nuts, a good year for babies'.

Now come all you jo-vial fel-lows, come lis-ten to my song. It is a lit-tle di-tty and it won't de-tain you long. It's of a fair young dam-sel, oh she lived down in Kent, a rose one sum-mer's mor-ning, and she a-nut-ting went. With a fal-lal to my ral-tal-lal Whack-fol-the-dear-ol-day, And what few nuts that poor girl had, she threw them all a-way.

It's of a brisk young farmer, was a-ploughing of his land,
He called unto his horses, and bid them gently stand.
As he sat down upon his plough, all for a song to sing,
His voice was so melodious, it made the valleys ring.

Chorus:
With a fal-lal to my ral-tal-lal
Whack-fol-the-dear-ol-day
And what few nuts that poor girl had
She threw them all away.

It's of this fair young damsel, she was nutting in the wood,
His voice was so melodious, it charmed her as she stood.
In that lonely wood, she could no longer stay,
And what few nuts she had, poor girl, she threw them all away.

Chorus

She then came to young Johnny, as he sat on his plough,
Said she, 'Young man, I really feel I cannot tell you how.'
He took her to some shady broom and there he laid her down,
Said she, 'Young man, I think I feel the
world go round and round.'

Chorus

So come all you young women, take warning by my song
If you should a-nutting go, don't stay from home too long.
For if you should stay too late, to hear the ploughboy sing,
You might have a young farmer to nurse up in the spring.

Chorus

September's Full Moon

Harvest Moon

The name Harvest Moon should be applied to the full moon that falls closest to the autumnal equinox. Most of the time that falls in September, but occasionally it will be the first of October's two full moons. Harvest time would have meant a great gathering of people pulled from neighbouring villages to do the most important farm job of the year in a short time, and those people needed to be fed, wined and entertained. The light of the full moon would have extended harvesting hours, as well as carousing ones.

A Song for September's Full Moon

'Autumn Comes, the Summer Is Past' ('Under the Harvest Moon')

Traditional, arr. Richard Barnard

This 16th-century English song, with its slightly mournful air, captures the feeling of summer slipping away under its golden light.

Au - tumn comes, the su - mmer is past,
Au - tumn comes, but let us be glad

Win - ter will come too soon.
Sing - ing an au - tumn tune.

Stars will shine clear - er, skies seem near - er
Hearts will be light - er, nights seem bright - er

Un - der the Har - vest Moon.
Un - der the Har - vest Moon.

A Hindu Tale for September

Ganesh and the Moon

The benevolent, wise, elephant-headed god Ganesh had a
terrible sweet tooth. One year on his birthday his devotees plied
him with his favourite sweet: modak, a delicious coconut- and
jaggery-filled dumpling. Ganesh could not resist: he ate and ate
until his belly was even fuller and rounder than it normally was,
and that was going some. Finally, he waddled off slowly through
the night, with more modak gathered up in his clothes. Now in
these days the moon shone full and bright all month long, but
despite his way being well lit, he tripped and fell, tearing his
clothes and scattering the sweets everywhere. The moon, who
was vain and regarded himself as very handsome, had always
thought Ganesh looked funny with his little short legs and his
big belly. When the moon saw Ganesh looking so undignified,
he fell about laughing and tears ran down his face, and this sent
the usually gentle Ganesh into a rage. 'How dare you laugh at
me?!' he bellowed. 'You think you are so beautiful! I curse you
to disappear from the sky and never show your face again!' The
moon was mortified: no one would ever see his handsome face
again? He begged Ganesh for mercy and Ganesh quickly
softened, but he knew that he could not take back his curse
completely. 'There will be only one day each month when you
vanish from the sky, and after that day you will grow until
you reach your full size, then shrink back to nothing again,'
he declared. And that is why the moon waxes and wanes.

Ganesh's birthday celebration, Ganesh Chaturthi, is held on
the fourth day of the Hindu month Bhadrapada. It is celebrated
with prayers, worship, processions and, of course, many sweets.
Ganesh is widely revered as the remover of obstacles, and as the
god of new beginnings and projects, making him the perfect
patron for September.

A Sea Shanty for September

'Ek Dam!'

Within Hinduism water is thought to activate luck and to cure problems, and this month for Ganesh Chaturthi – Ganesh's birthday – statues of the elephant god are carried in great processions to the sea and immersed. The most famous British example happens in Hounslow, west London, with Ganesh immersed in the River Thames. He is traditionally invoked before beginning journeys or new ventures.

To mark this, here is a rare example of a shanty in which Hindustani and pidgin English are mixed. Stan Hugill, in his book *Shanties from the Seven Seas*, says that he believes it would have originated among the lascars and khlassies, or Indian sailors, who worked the Nourse Line. These ships sailed from European ports, carrying a cargo of salt or steel to Calcutta. There they picked up indentured labourers and transported them to the Caribbean to carry out plantation work following the abolition of slavery in 1833. They then sailed up the American east coast and picked up grain, which they transported back to Europe.

Hugill knew the shanty as 'Eki-Duma' and thought this may be a corruption of the Hindustani expression *ek dom*, meaning 'one man', whereas the shanty singer Clint Hulton suggests that it comes from *ek-dam*, meaning 'one breath', or, effectively 'all together'. This was a halyard shanty, sung when hauling on a halyard (a rope, or line) to hoist a topsail, with the pull on the 'Ek'.

Kay kay kay kay! *Ek Dam!*
Kay kay kay kay! *Ek Dam!*

Sailorman no likee Bosun's Mate, Ek Dam!
Bosun's Mate no likee Head Serang, Ek Dam!
Head Serang no likee Number One, Ek Dam!
Number One no likee Khlassie Man, Ek Dam!

Kay kay kay kay! *Ek Dam!*
Kay kay kay kay! *Ek Dam!*

October

The Naming of October

Dàmhair (Scots Gaelic) | *October* (Scots/Ulster Scots)
Deireadh Fómhair (Irish Gaelic) | *Jerry-fouyir* (Manx)
Hydref (Welsh) | *Hedra* (Cornish) | *Octobre* (Jèrriais)
Putatengero (Romani)

The naming of this month in the languages of the British Isles gives glimpses into past autumnal concerns. Two are clear-cut: Deireadh Fómhair (Irish Gaelic) and Jerry-fouyir (Manx) both contain words meaning 'end' and 'harvest' – it is the final chance to gather in crops. But the Welsh Hydref (which is the Welsh word for both 'autumn' and 'October') is thought to be derived from *hydd* meaning 'stag' and *bref* meaning 'lowing, bleating', and the Cornish Hedra appears to come from the same root. The Scots Gaelic Dàmhair similarly points to the importance of deer in this month, and comes from *damh*, meaning 'rut'. It is rutting time, when the stags' bellows are heard at dawn and dusk – and the start of hunting season.

The 'month of the potatoes' was the final month of the big harvesting jobs for Romani families, and the 'tater picking up' was a big job to see them into the autumn. It was hard work, bending all day and then lifting the heavy loads of potatoes, but it was lucrative and carried out as the days turned increasingly cool and the leaves started to turn, the morning's fire suddenly particularly welcome to see off the night's chill and mists.

There is also a second and more controversial Welsh Romani name for October: Urchengero, month of the hedgehogs. Being marginalised from society, Romanies were forced either to live off wild things or to starve. It made them skilled trappers and hunters, making use of any wild food they could get hold of, catching rabbits and poaching pheasant for the pot.

Charm of the Month

Horseshoes

The tradition of hanging a horseshoe for good luck is particularly prevalent within the Gypsy and Roma communities, who have one of their major gatherings, the Stowe Horse Fair in Gloucester, this month. Horseshoe charms are worn as jewellery by the women of the communities, and real horseshoes hang above the doors to wagons and caravans.

The tale goes that a Roma man was riding back to his camp one night when he found himself being pursued by four demons: bad luck, ill health, unhappiness and death. He raced ahead of them but bad luck started to catch up, at which point the man's horse's shoe flew off, hit bad luck on the head, and killed him. The three demons retreated to bury their brother and the man returned for the horseshoe, then hung it up above his wagon door to show that it had killed bad luck.

Finding one on the roadside is the luckiest way to get your own. Always hang a horseshoe with the ends pointing upwards, to hold in the luck. A horseshoe is also useful up the chimney to prevent witches flying down it.

Dressing Up in October

Pearly Kings and Queens

On the first Sunday in October, the Pearly Kings and Queens of St Pancras hold their Harvest Festival at St Martin-in-the-Fields. Another Pearly Harvest Festival is held in late September at the Guildhall Yard and St Mary-le-Bow. Both are great gatherings of Pearlies in all their finery.

Harvest and fresh produce are at the core of Pearly history. Their story begins with the costermongers, who have traded in London for up to a thousand years. The word comes from Costard, a widely available variety of apple in medieval times, and monger, which meant 'seller'. In fact, these traders sold all sorts of fresh produce in the streets and alleyways, first from barrows and later from market stalls, mostly serving the poor who could only afford to buy in small amounts and wouldn't have been welcomed in the shops. They hawked their wares with distinctive cries, much to the annoyance of well-to-do society, and became known for their style and panache, their use of slang and their love of ale houses, gin palaces and music halls – cosy places to be when lodgings were so often grim.

Costermongers were often unlicensed, itinerant traders, and despite the essential service they provided, they were much harassed by the authorities. As London grew, the costermongers elected a 'coster king' and often a 'coster queen' from each borough to fight for their rights – a sort of early trade union rep. The kings and queens also raised money for fellow costermongers who had fallen on hard times, and for the London poor they saw all around them. In time, the 'royal' children of the coster kings and queens inherited their titles and charitable duties.

The costume came in the 1880s when road-sweeper and rat-catcher Henry Croft, a friend and admirer of the costers, found a stash of smoked pearl buttons and used them to decorate a worn-out suit and top hat with the words 'All For Charity'. The costers loved to wear pearls to emulate the clothing of wealthy West End society and they quickly followed Croft's example, the women adding ostrich feathers, the men pearling working caps and waistcoats. To this day they continue to raise huge sums of money for charity, while looking very dapper indeed.

Folk Song of the Month

'The Costermonger's Song'

Traditional, arr. Richard Barnard

The costermongers were known for their vibrant pub culture. The original music hall venues of the 1830s were 'song and supper rooms' in the saloon bars of public houses. Created so that the working classes could eat, drink and smoke while being entertained, they were very different from the more genteel, middle-class theatres. Many of the songs were bawdy and rousing, written to be sung along to at top volume. 'Coster songs' such as this were sung in an exaggerated Cockney accent, and often featured mentions of the wares they sold.

I'm Billy Bell, a coster-monger, you sees,
A-selling of potatoes, leeks and cabbages,
Artichokes and cauliflowers; I thinks that I can say
I deals in everything what's in the vegetable way.
And though I work so very hard, I has me pleasure too
For every Derby Day away to Epsom I would go.

Going to the Derby looking very smart,
Doing all the journey in me donkey cart.
Passing all the vehicles, turning in and out,
Going to the Derby in me little donkey cart.

And when I gets to Epsom amongst the bustle there
I puts away me donkey what hasn't turned a hair.
Then I gets me luncheon: a chunk of bread and cheese,
A gallon jar of fourpenny, at which you wouldn't sneeze.
And if I've won a bob or two, I has an happy heart
Returning from the Derby in my little donkey cart.

Going to the Derby looking very smart,
Doing all the journey in me donkey cart.
Passing all the vehicles, turning in and out,
Going to the Derby in me little donkey cart.

A Welsh Folk Tale for October

Merlin's Apples

There are many real-world candidates for the legendary Isle of Apples of Arthurian legend, widely known as the Isle of Avalon (derived from *afal*, Welsh for 'apple'). One such is Ynys Enlli, or Bardsey Island, off the tip of the Llŷn Peninsula in Gwynned, Wales. Here it is said that the wizard Merlin lived in a magical glass castle, and Morgan le Fay – the healer and enchantress, and King Arthur's half-sister – studied under him. Apples often play a magical role in folk tales and myths, the trees being gateways to fairy lands or the underworld, and the apples themselves poisoned or enchanted. Avalon was one such gateway, and the trees on its slopes produced fruit all year round. Morgan brought Arthur to Avalon when he was mortally wounded, and he was either laid to rest, or – in keeping with the apple island's powers – he still awaits the moment for his messianic return, to claim the throne.

In 1998 a keen ornithologist, Andy Clarke, was on Bardsey Island to catch and ring birds. Needing bait for his net, he collected some windfall apples under a gnarled tree in the lee of an old house. He noticed that, unusually for north Wales, the apples were disease-free, so he sent samples to the National Fruit Collection at Brogdale in Kent. They pronounced them unique: no one had seen this apple before. Cuttings were taken and Bardsey Island Apple Trees can now be bought, in small quantities. The apple is rosy in colour and tastes lemony and sweet; it cooks to a light golden fluff. Locals say that the tree has always been there, and they know the apples as 'Merlin's apples'. There is a theory that the myth of the glass castle arose from some kind of early greenhouse that allowed apples to thrive in Bardsey's harsh conditions.

Apple Day falls on 21st October. Started in 1990 by the charity Common Ground, it was created as an opportunity to celebrate the rich history and variety of apples in the British Isles. Look out for local orchard events.

Folk Story of the Month

The Peddler of Swaffham

The peddler in this story does not take his wares to London, but he finds his fortune there anyway, in a roundabout way.

There was once a poor peddler who lived in Swaffham in Norfolk. Every day he would buy produce from the market gardens and pick apples from his own orchard, and then hawk them in the streets and marketplace. One night he had a vivid dream that he was standing on London Bridge. This was in the days when London Bridge was lined with shops from one end to the other, and in the dream he was surrounded by noise and bustle. As he stood outside a haberdasher's shop on the bridge, he was told the most wonderful news. But when he woke up he could no longer remember what it was. The following night he had the dream again, and the next night he had it yet again. When he woke on the third morning, he decided he had to walk to London and see if he could find out what this news might be.

When he arrived at London Bridge, all looked just as it had in his dream. He heard the cries of the costermongers – 'Penny a lot, fine russets!' and 'Four bunches a penny: water cresses'. He walked up and down the bridge all day long, but he was none the wiser. The next day he did the same, with the same result. On the third day a shopkeeper stepped out of his haberdashery shop and hailed him. 'I have seen you walking here these past few days,' said the shopkeeper. 'You have no goods to sell and you are not begging. What is your business?' The peddler told him about his dream, at which the shopkeeper laughed. 'You are a fool to come all this way because of a dream,' he said. 'Why, I too have had a dream every night for the past week, that there is a pot of gold hidden under an apple tree in a town called Swaffham that I have never visited and never intend to visit. Be off home with you!' The peddler did exactly as he was told, and walked all the way home. In his orchard he dug up the gold, which kept him in fine style for the rest of his days.

October's Full Moon

Hunter's Moon | Blood Moon

The Hunter's Moon or Blood Moon is named in praise of its helpful rays, suggesting the creation of perfect hunting and slaughtering conditions.

A Song for October's Full Moon

'The Wild, Wild Berry'

Traditional, arr. Richard Barnard

Young man came from hunting faint and wea-ry,

"Oh, what ails my son, my dea-ry?" "Oh, mo-ther dear, let my

bed be made for I feel the gripe of the woo-dy night-shade."

Lie low, sweet Ran-dall. Now, all you young men that do

eat full well, and you that sups right me-rry, 'tis a far be-tter treat to have

toads for your meat than to eat of the wild, wild be-rry.

This song is for the hunter's moon – a dark and eerie thing. The song goes by many different titles and has varying lyrics, but the gist is always that a young man comes home from hunting in the moonlight beset by terrible pains, having met with his false love, who has poisoned him with deadly nightshade in order to be rid of him.

> Young man came from hunting faint and weary,
> 'Oh, what ails my son, my deary?'
> 'Oh, mother dear, let my bed be made,
> For I feel the gripe of the woody nightshade.'
> Lie low, sweet Randall.

> *Chorus:*
> *Now all you young men that do eat full well,*
> *And you that sups right merry:*
> *'Tis a far better treat to have toads for your meat*
> *Than to eat of the wild, wild berry.*

> Now this young man, well, he died full soon
> By the light of the hunter's moon.
> Not by the bolt, nor yet by blade
> But the gripe of the woody nightshade.
> Lie low, sweet Randall.

> *Chorus*

> The lordship's love they hanged her high,
> For she had caused her lord to die.
> In her hair they entwined a braid
> Of the leaves and berries of the woody nightshade.
> Lie low, sweet Randall.

> *Chorus*

A Sea Shanty for October

'Roll the Cotton Down'

A shanty to mark Black History Month, which has been observed in the United Kingdom since 1987. As Stan Hugill states in his book *Shanties of the Seven Seas*, a great number of shanties have clear origins as the working songs of slaves on plantations in the American South and the West Indies. Indeed, the very notion of singing while working was an intrinsic part of African culture.

In the Southern port city of Mobile, Alabama, African American slaves – and, later, former slaves – worked packing the cotton onto ships bound for Europe, a hugely physical and demanding job. They were often joined in this work by English and Irish sailors, who sometimes overwintered in Mobile to avoid sailing during the treacherous North Atlantic winter. The African Americans sang songs as they worked, and these songs were picked up by the European sailors, sometimes in their entirety but often as fragments with their own words added later. There was a great flourishing of musical cross-pollination, with a particular wealth of Irish and African American crossovers, such as the words of an Irish song being set to the tune of an African American one. All was tumbled about in the great musical melting pot that was the Atlantic Ocean between 1815 and 1860, the age of merchant sailing ships and of sea shanties.

This shanty is pretty clearly of African American origin. It is a t'gallant halyard shanty, used when hauling the t'gallant halyard (rope, or line) to set the topgallant sail. The job needed a lively, quick beat, which this song provides if sung at a marching pace.

♩ = 60

Oh, way down south where I was born *Roll the cot-ton down!* Oh, I worked in the cot-ton and I worked in the corn *We'll roll the cot-ton down!* Roll the cot-ton! *Roll the cot-ton,* *Mo-ses!* Roll the cot-ton! *We'll roll the cot-ton down!*

Around Cape Horn we're bound to go
Roll the cotton down!
Around Cape Stiff through ice and snow
We'll roll the cotton down!
Roll the cotton!
Roll the cotton, Moses!
Roll the cotton!
We'll roll the cotton down!

We're bound away at the break of day
Roll the cotton down!
And come back here to Mobile Bay
We'll roll the cotton down!...

Oh, Mobile Bay's no place for me
Roll the cotton down!
I'll sail away on some other sea
We'll roll the cotton down!...

Pilgrimage of the Month

Trick-or-Treating

Trick-or-treating is a ritual journey passed down through the ages, albeit a pretty short journey that is mostly about fun and sweets. On Hallowe'en we dress up and parade around our neighbourhoods, a small and spooky annual pilgrimage.

The 31st October has always been associated with the supernatural, though it is unclear exactly why. We know that the 1st November was the festival of Samhain and was considered the first day of winter, and so on the 31st October, end-of-summer feasts and celebrations were held throughout Britain and Ireland. Such shifts from one season to the next have always been considered the times when fairies, goblins, trolls and witches were at their most active. In addition, the coldest, darkest times of the year were approaching, and hence the time of year likely to see the most deaths, and the countryside around reflected this in dying back and withering. Divination rituals – mainly revolving around who was going to die next – were a major part of Samhain Eve celebrations, perhaps because of this. All of these elements may have fed into the night's spooky associations, when it was thought pertinent to avoid churchyards and crossroads, places where spooks would be most likely to gather.

The origins of trick-or-treating itself lie in the far north of Scotland and in Ireland, where Samhain Eve was sometimes known as Puca Night, or Goblin Night. The practice of dressing up and parading, holding carved vegetable lamps, originated with mummers. Mimicking the very ghouls that everyone was scared of and parading around the neighbourhood was thought to scare them away. Following mass Irish emigration during Victorian times, the practice began to spread throughout Scotland, Wales and northern England and, of course, into America. From there it was imported – pumpkins and all – back to Britain and Ireland via popular culture.

A Song for Hallowe'en

'Soul Cake'

Traditional

A soul, a soul, a soul - cake, Please, good miss - us a soul - cake, An apple, a pear, a plum or a cher - ry, A - ny good thing to make us all mer - ry. One for Pet - er, two for Paul, Three for Him that made us all.

From medieval times right up to the 1930s, children went a-souling door to door on Hallowe'en. This was the song they sang in the hope of winning a soul cake or two from their neighbours.

God bless the master of this house and the mistress also
And all the little children that around your table grow,
Likewise your men and maidens, your cattle and your store
And all that dwells within your gates,
We wish you ten times more.

Chorus:
A soul, a soul, a soul cake,
Please, good missus, a soul cake,
An apple, a pear, a plum or a cherry,
Any good thing to make us all merry.
One for Peter, two for Paul,
Three for Him that made us all.

The lanes are very dirty and my shoes are very thin,
I've got a little pocket I can put a penny in.
If you haven't got a penny, a ha'penny will do,
If you haven't got a ha'penny, then God bless you.

November

The Naming of November

Samhain (Scots Gaelic) | *November* (Scots/Ulster Scots)
Samhain (Irish Gaelic) | *Mee Houney* (Manx)
Tachwed (Welsh) | *Du* (Cornish) | *Novembre* (Jèrriais)
Bare-machengero (Romani)

The pre-Christian Celtic year began on 1st November, with the festival of Samhain, one of the four markers of the Celtic year (the others being Imbolc, Beltane and Lughnasadh). Samhain marks the beginning of winter and was the time the cattle were brought in from the pastures to their winter quarters. The word may be derived from the Proto-Indo-European *sam*, meaning 'together'. Samhain was considered a time when the spirits of the dead could return to the earth, with the veil between the living and the dead especially thin. The word for November in Scots Gaelic and Irish Gaelic is Samhain, while the Manx name, Mee Houney, is derived from it.

The Welsh Tachwed takes a different direction and means 'slaughter' (much as the Anglo-Saxon word for November was *Blotmonath*, meaning 'blood month'). This is because November was the traditional time to slaughter and preserve the meat of farm animals, fattened up over summer. The Cornish name, Du, again leans towards the Breton name for the month (also *Du*) and means 'black', perhaps related to the shortening days.

For Welsh Romani and Scottish Travellers, this month held a special wild harvest, so good and abundant that the month was named after it – month of the salmon. As the rivers were running with salmon, salmon poaching would be commonplace in November, with the fishing done by moonlight or in out-of-the-way corners of rivers to avoid gamekeepers. The Welsh Romanies in particular have always been good fishermen, and would fish Bala Lake in Snowdonia for pike, perch, brown trout, roach and eel. All would be brought back to the fire to be cooked and shared among the family and anyone else who came by, making a rare quick meal to replace the usual slow-cooked stews.

A Sea Shanty for November

'The Fishes'

A sea shanty for the salmon migration taking place around the coast and up the rivers this month. This is a tops'l halyard shanty, used when the rope (the halyard) that raised a topsail needed to be hauled, hence its simple rhythmic nature.

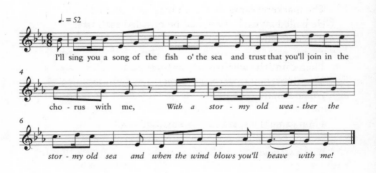

I'll sing you a song of the fish o' the sea and trust that you'll join in the chorus with me, With a stor - my old wea - ther the stor - my old sea and when the wind blows you'll heave with me!

There once was a skipper, I don't know his name,
But I know that he played a very smart game.
With a stormy old weather the stormy old sea
And when the wind blows you'll heave with me!

When his ship lay becalmed in the tropical sea,
He whistled all day but he could get no breeze.
With a stormy...

Up leaped a salmon as bright as the sun,
He jumped between decks and then fired off a gun.
With a stormy...

Then came the eel with his slippery tail,
He climbed up aloft and he cast off each sail.
With a stormy...

The mackerel came then with his pretty striped back,
He hailed aft each sheet, and he boarded each tack.
With a stormy...

Then came the whale who was biggest at sea,
Shouting 'Haul in yer head sheets, now, hellums a-lee!'
With a stormy...

Then came the sprat, he was smallest of all,
He jumped on the poop cryin' 'Maintawps'l haul!'
With a stormy...

Last came the herring, the King of the Sea,
He looked at the men and said 'Captain I'll be!'
With a stormy...

The breeze it blew hard, and they sailed 'cross the sea,
Oh, what a smart captain that captain must be!
With a stormy...

A Christian Tale for November

All Saints, All Souls and Remembrance

In 3rd-century Rome, Christians were not welcome. The Roman people found converts to this almost new religion threatening and unsettling. Why wouldn't they make animal sacrifices like everybody else? Why did they worship secretly in their own homes? And worst of all, why was their loyalty to their God and not to the Roman state? They were seen as corrosive to society and were blamed for natural disasters: if you do not worship the pantheon of Roman gods correctly, what do you expect to happen?

Persecution was common but piecemeal and often mob-led, and the death of each Christian martyr was marked by the Christian community annually. And then along came Decius, Roman emperor from 249 to 251. He issued a decree requiring Christians to carry out a public act of sacrifice as a testimony of allegiance to the empire. Refusal was punished by imprisonment, torture and execution.

Yet many refused, and the number of martyrs grew so great that it became impossible to mark the date of each martyrdom. The Christian Church adopted a common day for all: the Feast of All Saints, or All Saints' Day. This was at first celebrated annually on 13th May but later was moved to 1st November by Pope Gregory III in the 8th century. It then coincided – deliberately perhaps – with the Celtic pagan celebration of Samhain, which is itself a commemoration of the dead, of lost relatives and friends, and is considered a time when the veil between the worlds of the living and the dead is at its thinnest.

In the 11th century, 2nd November was chosen as All Souls' Day, a day to remember all of the faithful who have died. And later still, early November became the time to remember another mass loss of life – in World War I – on Remembrance Day and Remembrance Sunday. It seems that these quiet, dark moments in the year lend themselves to contemplation, appreciation and commemoration of lost loved ones.

A Song for Remembrance

'Far, Far from Wipers'

Most of the songs of World War I came out of music halls,
and their purpose was to keep spirits up and morale high
among those waiting back at home. The soldiers in the
trenches sang their own songs, most often new words set
to well-known tunes and hymns, and again they generally
had a jaunty air, albeit with a little bit of very British
comedy grumbling. Very few gave any hint of the actual
horrors endured, and with good reason: their purpose was
to help the men keep on, not to encourage them to sink
into despair. 'Far, Far from Wipers' is one of the few with
a plaintive air and a good dose of reality, short as it is.
'Wipers' was what the British soldiers called the northern
French town of Ypres (actually pronounced 'Eep') which
was where some of the worst fighting of the war took place.

Far, far from Wipers I long to be, Where
German snipers can't get at me. Damp is
my dug out, cold are my feet, wait-ing for
whizz bangs to send me to sleep.

Charm of the Month

Pudding Charms

The last Sunday before Advent is Stir-up Sunday, the day we must all get our puddings underway if they are to be suitably matured and brandy-soaked by Christmas Day. (It's a good day to make your Christmas cake and mincemeat, too, for the same reason.) This is the last Sunday before Advent, and the name comes from the beginning of the Anglican Church's prayer for the day: 'Stir up, we beseech thee, oh Lord, the wills of thy faithful people.' Of course this has nothing whatsoever to do with puddings, but a necessary task and a handily timed Bible reading have become conjoined over the years. A Christmas pudding should contain exactly 13 ingredients, to represent Jesus and the disciples. It should be stirred from east to west to represent the journey of the Magi. Each member of the family should stir it and make a wish as they do so. In what is thought to possibly be a hangover of far older charm traditions associated with Epiphany, silver charms were once included at this stage, and each represented a different facet of luck for the year ahead: a silver sixpence for wealth, a ring for love and marriage, and a thimble for luck.

The Laird of Balmachie's Wife

We think of fairies as sweet, happy little creatures but in the past it was well understood that they were wicked. They were particularly known for swapping healthy human babies for their own sickly changelings. Luckily, fairy folk that are up to no good can be stopped by being thrown onto the fire. No effigies for them – on they go, shawl, bonnet and all. This is what happens in this tale from Dumfries and Galloway in Scotland.

Many years ago, the Laird of Balmachie was required to ride to Dundee on business. His wife was ill and so stayed at home in bed. As the laird was returning, dusk was falling, so he took a short cut in order to reach home before dark. As he rode along, he spotted a troop of fairies on the hillside, carrying a sedan chair. He sensed that they were up to no good, so he drew his sword and galloped up the hillside after them, shouting, 'In the name of God, release your captive!' The tiny troop and chair vanished and a woman fell into the damp heather. Rushing over, the laird was astonished to see that it was his own wife, dressed in her nightclothes, confused and chilly but otherwise unhurt.

They rode back to their castle and the lady went to bed in a warm bedroom. He then went to her bedchamber, where he had left her that morning. There he found a very sickly and pale version of his wife, sitting there complaining about how she had been neglected and cold all day. 'Here, wife, let me build up the fire for you,' said the laird, and he heaped logs onto the fire until it was roaring. 'Now, come a little closer to the fire and we will warm you up,' said the laird. The lady refused, and so the laird lifted her out of bed, carried her to the fire and threw her onto it. She landed in the flames and then immediately flew straight up into the air, bursting a hole in the roof.

Fairies were never seen again around the laird's house, but although the hole in the roof was well mended, once each year a great wind would blow up that would damage that one piece, and no other, requiring it to be mended all over again.

Folk Song of the Month

'Cob-Coaling'

Traditional, arr. Richard Barnard

This Bonfire Night song is from the Lancashire and Yorkshire
border and is thought to have once been part of a mummers'
play. It refers to the tradition of cob-coaling in the run-up to
Bonfire Night, when children went from door to door singing
cob-coaling songs to ask for lumps of wood and coal, and
money for fireworks. The practice of cob-coaling is thought to
have died out in the 1980s. More recently, however, it was a
street song, sometimes sung by children asking for 'a penny for
the Guy' as they carted around an effigy of Guy Fawkes they'd
made from old rags, which would eventually be thrown on the
bonfire – another custom that has generally disappeared. The
song contains a snippet of the nursery rhyme 'Remember,
Remember the Fifth of November', which is still chanted by
the Lewes Bonfire Societies.

> We come a cob-coaling for Bonfire Time,
> Your coal and your money we hope you enjoy.
> *Fal-a-dee, fal-a-die, fal-a-diddle-die-do-day*
>
> Now down in your cellar there's an old umbrella,
> There's nowt in yon corner but an old pepper box.
> Pepper box, pepper box, morning till night;
> If you give us nowt, we'll take nowt
> and bid you good night!
> *Fol-a-dee, fol-a-die, fol-a-diddle-die-do-day*
>
> Remember, remember the fifth of November
> For gunpowder, treason should never be forgot.
> We'll knock at your knocker and ring at your bell
> and see what you give us for singing so well.
> *Fol-a-dee, fol-a-die, fol-a-diddle-die-do-day*

November's Full Moon

Darkest Depths Moon
Moon Before Yule | Mourning Moon

As we tip further away from the sun, the nights lengthen and turn colder, and frosts become increasingly likely. There is every chance that the light from November's full moon will fall upon a gently glittering countryside. The name Darkest Depths Moon is a nice case of stating the obvious, albeit poetically. We are nearly at the very darkest point in the year, and the nights are long and cold; clearly pointing this out once felt pretty important. Moon Before Yule is even more self-evident, but Mourning Moon is something of a puzzle. Perhaps this was connected to the ancient Celtic festival of Samhain or the Christian All Souls' Day, both of which have at their hearts a commemoration of those who have passed away, or perhaps it is a sad farewell to the growing year.

A Song for November's Full Moon

'Van Diemen's Land'

Traditional, arr. Richard Barnard

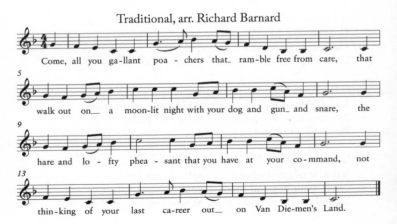

Come, all you gallant poachers that ramble free from care, that walk out on a moonlit night with your dog and gun and snare, the hare and lofty pheasant that you have at your command, not thinking of your last career out on Van Diemen's Land.

In this song our poor heroes set out under the moonlight to go poaching but are caught red-handed. The rest of the song follows their transportation to Australia's principal 19th-century penal colony in Van Diemen's Land, as the Australian island of Tasmania was called then.

Come, all you gallant poachers that ramble free from care,
That walk out on a moonlit night with
your dog, and gun and snare,
The hare and lofty pheasant you have at your command,
Not thinking of your last career out on Van Diemen's Land.

Me and two more went out one night to Squire Daniel's park,
To see if we could catch some game, the night it being dark,
But to our great misfortune we felt the keeper's hand,
Our sentence was for fourteen years upon Van Diemen's Land.

Oh, when we came to land there, upon that fatal shore,
The planters they came flocking round, full twenty score or more,
They ranked us up like horses and sold us out of hand,
They yoked us up with heavy chains to plough Van Diemen's Land.

I often look behind me towards my native shore,
And dream of my old cottage that I shall see no more,
With my true love beside me and a jug of ale in hand,
But wake quite broken-hearted out in Van Diemen's Land.

So come, you gallant poachers, give ear unto my song,
It is a bit of good advice although it is not long,
Lay by your dog and snare, to you I do speak plain.
If you knew our great hardships, you'd never poach again.

DECEMBER

ME-DEBLESKO MUNTHOS

MY GOD'S MONTH

XII

December

The Naming of December

Dùbhlachd (Scots Gaelic)
December (Scots/Ulster Scots)
Nollaig (Irish Gaelic)
Mee ny Nollick (Manx) | *Rhagfyr* (Welsh)
Kevardhu (Cornish) | *Dézembre* (Jèrriais)
Me-deblesko munthos (Romani)

Nollaig (Irish Gaelic) and Mee ny Nollick (Manx) both come from *natalicius*, Latin for 'birthday' or 'birth'. Relating to Christmas, this is the only place where Christianity has left its mark on the names of the month in the languages of the British Isles, and it suggests that these particular names are not as ancient as some. The Welsh Rhagyr means 'foreshortening' and is thought to relate to the shortening of days. In a similar vein, the Scots Gaelic Dùbhlachd, meaning 'black', is concerned with the increasing gloom. Cornish goes one step further, having used up 'black' on November; its name for December is Kevardhu (which is most similar to the Breton name for the month, *Kerzu*) and means 'very black'.

The Romani name for December – 'my god's month' – is a clear reference to Christmas and the birth of Jesus. There is no single religion within Romani culture, and depending on where they have travelled, some Romanies have adopted Islam and others have retained a faith in Hinduism that they may have brought with them from roots in India. But the vast majority are Christians, and almost all British and Irish Romanies are.

Full Cold Moon | Oak Moon
Moon After Yule

December's Full Cold Moon is the highest and brightest of the year. In the year-round wrestle for dominion that is played out in the sky between the sun and the moon, the moon is definitely winning right now, and shines high, bright and strong over the winter countryside, just as the sun stays low and weak. But, of course, December brings the winter solstice, the moment at which the pendulum starts to swing back the other way. Neopagans believe that in pre-Christian times, the year was ruled over by two kings, the Holly King from the summer solstice to the winter solstice, and the Oak King, from winter to summer. They had to do battle for supremacy, and the winter solstice was the moment at which the Oak King slayed the Holly King and – like the sun – started to build strength. Perhaps this is some clue to the origin of the name Oak Moon.

A Song for December's Full Moon
'The Moon Shines Bright'

Traditional, arr. Richard Barnard

This beautiful old country carol was originally collected by folk song collector Lucy Broadwood from Gypsy singers in Suffolk and Surrey around 1900, and is thought to have medieval origins. It was most likely sung by wassailers, who went from house to house like today's carol singers.

The moon shines bright and the stars give a light
A little before the day.
The Lord our God, he calls on us
And bids us awake and pray.

So for the saving of our souls
Christ died upon the cross.
We ne'er shall do for Jesus Christ
What he has done for us.

The life of man, it is but a span
And cut down like a flower.
For he's here today, but tomorrow he is gone
And dead all in an hour.

The clock strikes one, and it's time we were gone,
We'll stay no longer here.
God bless you all, both great and small
And send you a happy New Year.

A Sea Shanty for December

'Rolling Home'

One of many superstitions attached to shantying was that songs about setting out should be sung only on the outward journey and songs about coming home only on the inward one. This forebitter (a song sung in the sailors' leisure time) sees our sailors starting for home from Australia, sailing right around the world, and eventually being lit along the south coast and into port by the lighthouses of the Lizard, Start Point, Eddystone, Portland Bill and Dover. A fitting end to our year of shanties.

To Australia's lovely daughters,
We will bid a fond adieu,
For we're bound for dear Old England
To return no more to you.

> *Rolling home, rolling home,*
> *Rolling home across the sea,*
> *Rolling home to dear Old England,*
> *Rolling home, fair land, to thee.*

Up aloft amidst the rigging
Blows the wild and rushing gale,
Straining every spar and backstay,
Spreading out each swelling sail.

> *Rolling home...*

Cheer up, Jack, bright smiles await you
From the fairest of the fair,
There are loving hearts to greet you
With kind welcomes everywhere.

> *Rolling home...*

And we'll sing the joyful chorus
In the watches of the night,
And we'll see the shores of England
When the grey dawn brings the light.

> *Rolling home...*

A Polish Christmas Story for December

Wigilia and the Animals

On Christmas Eve at the stroke of midnight, something magical happens in barns, hutches and dog baskets. For one hour only, it is said that animals are given the power of human speech, although only those who have led a blameless life can hear them. This ability is bestowed upon them because of the part they played in the stable in Bethlehem, watching over Jesus in the manger. The ox and the donkey are the only ones that get a Bible mention, and they bowed down to him. But the shepherds must have brought their sheep, and what stable doesn't have a few mice running around in the straw, or a pair of doves in the rafters, or maybe even a small colony of overwintering bees in the cracks between the stones? Christmas lore around the British Isles has it that bees wake from their winter slumber to hum Psalm 100, 'Make a Joyful Noise Unto the Lord'. But such festive animal tales are most widespread in continental Europe, and they have been fully interwoven into Polish Christmas traditions.

Polish families celebrate on Christmas Eve, known as *Wigilia*, meaning 'vigil'. The meal can only begin when the first star of the evening is spotted in the sky, and it always begins with the breaking and sharing of *oplatek*, a thin wafer, pieces of which are also given to each pet or farm animal. The meal comprises 12 courses, one for each of the disciples, and is meat-free, partly in recognition of the animals. Straw is placed under the table or under the tablecloth to remind people of the stable.

Poles have long made up the UK's largest foreign-born and second-generation population, partly because Polish military units based themselves in Britain during Nazi occupation of Poland, and were encouraged to stay after the war in recognition of their war contribution. A great many households around Britain will be looking out for the first star this Christmas Eve.

Charm of the Month

The Wishbone

After Christmas dinner, the turkey's wishbone – the V-shaped bone above its breastbone – is taken out, cleaned and left to dry, which will be faster if placed by the fire. As soon as it is nicely dried out, it is ready to be used. Two people – usually chosen from the children at the table – face off, make a wish and wrap their pudgy pinkies around a side each, then pull until it snaps. The one left holding the longest end wins, and their wish will come true (this is thought to be the origin of the term 'lucky break'). Traditions around the wishbone are found in many cultures. Prussian and Celtic armies used wishbones to predict the weather, and the ancient Etruscans once used the movements and bones of birds for divination, and would dry out the wishbone and stroke it while making wishes. The Romans took the tradition from the Etruscans and spread it around their empire. In Britain the bone took on (and later lost) the name 'merrythought' and became part of the Christmas ritual. Eventually it went across the Atlantic to the United States, where there are, of course, plentiful wild turkeys. Although in the US the turkey, along with its wishbone, is principally connected with Thanksgiving, in the UK it has become most strongly associated with the Christmas turkey.

A Song for Christmas
'The Friendly Beasts'

Traditional

This carol seems to have originated in France but was
well known in England from the 12th century, though
this form of words may be more modern. It lets the
animals in the stable tell their own story of the nativity.

Je - sus our bro - ther, strong and good, was hum - bly

born in a sta - ble rude, and the friend - ly beasts a -

round him stood, Je - sus our bro - ther, strong and good.

'I' said the donkey, shaggy and brown,
'I carried his mother up hill and down;
I carried his mother to Bethlehem town.'
'I' said the donkey, shaggy and brown.

'I' said the cow, all white and red
'I gave him my manger for his bed;
I gave him my hay to pillow his head.'
'I' said the cow, all white and red.

'I' said the sheep with curly horn,
'I gave him my wool for his blanket warm;
He wore my coat on Christmas morn.'
'I' said the sheep with curly horn.

'I' said the dove from the rafters high,
'I cooed him to sleep so that he would not cry;
We cooed him to sleep, my mate and I.'
'I' said the dove from the rafters high.

Thus every beast by some good spell
In the stable dark was glad to tell
Of the gift he gave Emmanuel,
The gift he gave Emmanuel.

**COLLARED
DOVE**

Dressing Up in December

The 'Wren Boys' of Ireland

On St Stephen's Day, 26th December, in towns and villages along the west coast of Ireland, people will dress up in straw suits and hats that cover their faces to 'hunt the wren'. Although no birds are now harmed, wrens were once actually hunted as part of the custom. Tied to the end of a long pole, they were carried through the streets as the bearers knocked on doors and asked for money to bury the wren. The donors would receive a feather from the bird, for luck, as sailors and fishermen believed that those who possessed a wren's feather would never be shipwrecked. Traditionally, this money was used to throw a 'Wren's Ball', sometime in January.

The hunting of the wren is a curiously widespread custom, most common in Ireland but with variants on the Isle of Man and in Pembrokeshire, as well as in southern France and Galicia in northwest Spain. This is particularly odd as throughout Europe wrens have long been considered lucky and sacred – they are called king of the birds in several European languages – and to kill one was thought to bring bad luck. Nobody quite knows what it all means, but there are plenty of theories.

The wren has long been associated with winter because it sings on through the darkest months. This led to a belief that it could be slain and brought back to life, a symbol – much like the evergreen foliage with which we deck our halls – of the triumph of light over darkness, and life over death. The Celtic name for wren is *dreoilín*, which some have conjectured could come from *draoi ean*, or 'druid's bird', so perhaps the tradition arose from some sort of ritualised sacrifice. Wrens also represent the old year, so this may be the logic behind killing one as the year ends. On yet another hand, it may have arisen because it was the wren that betrayed St Stephen to his enemies by singing in the bush in which he was hiding (*dreoilín* also means 'trickster').

Now, happily, a stuffed or fake wren, adorned with ribbons is tied to a holly bush on a stick. It is carried from door to door while the 'wren boys' sing and dance and collect money. A tradition steeped in mystery, to end the year.

Folk Story of the Month

How the Wren Became King of the Birds

Despite its diminutive size, the wren is known as the king of the birds, and is also considered tricky and cunning, perhaps partly because of its ability to quickly flit and disappear into a hedgerow. Here is how it got its name, and its reputation.

Once upon a time, all of the birds gathered together for a race to decide who among them was king of the birds. It was decided that whichever bird could fly the highest would be crowned. They all took off in a great beating of wings, flying straight upwards towards the sun. Up and up they flew, but soon the smaller birds were exhausted, as their little wings had beaten so many times, and they fell away from the pack and flew back down to earth. Gradually the ducks, the gulls, the crows and even the owls drifted back down to the ground, defeated. And so it went on until there was one single huge eagle still beating its wings skyward. Finally, worn out and triumphant, he started to glide downwards, at which the little wren popped out from where he had been clinging onto the underside of one of the eagle's wings. Entirely rested from hitching a ride, he flew up above the exhausted eagle, who now had no energy to fly any higher, and sang, 'I am the king! I am the king!'

All of the birds were astonished when they heard the news, as they hadn't expected so tiny a bird to win. The eagle was furious. 'I used all of my strength to win,' he said. 'I should be king!' But the wren said, 'If the eagle can win through his strength, why can I not win through my cunning and cleverness?' And so the matter was settled.

Folk Song of the Month

'The Wren Song'

Traditional, arr. Richard Barnard

This is the song sung by the 'wren boys' as they parade the streets on St Stephen's Day, 26th December. Wren is pronounced 'wran'.

Fast ♩. = 132

The wren, the wren, the king of all birds St Ste-phen's Day was caught in the furze. Al-though he was lit-tle his ho-nour was great, jump up, my lads and give us a treat. As I was go-ing to Kil-le-naule I met a wren u-pon a wall, up with my wat-tle and knocked him down and brought him in to Car-rick Town. "Dreoi-lín, dreoi-lín. where's your nest?" "Tis in the bush that I love best; in the tree,_ the hol-ly tree, where all the boys do fol-low me." *Up with the ket-tle and down with the pan and give us a pen-ny to bu-ry the wren.*

The wren, the wren, the king of all birds
St Stephen's Day was caught in the furze,
Although he was little his honour was great,
Jump up, my lads and give us a treat.

As I was going to Killenaule,
I met a wren upon a wall,
Up with my wattle and knocked him down
And brought him in to Carrick Town.

'Dreoilín, dreoilín, where's your nest?'
"Tis in the bush that I love best;
In the tree, the holly tree,
Where all the boys do follow me.'
Up with the kettle and down with the pan
And give us a penny to bury the wren.

I followed the wren three miles or more,
Three miles or more, three miles or more
I followed the wren three miles or more
At six-o-clock in the morning.

I have a box here under my arm,
Here under my arm, here under my arm.
I have a box here under my arm,
A penny or tuppence would do it no harm.

Mrs Quinn's a very good woman
A very good woman, a very good woman
Mrs Quinn's a very good woman
She'll give us a penny to bury the wren.
Up with the kettle and down with the pan
And give us a penny to bury the wren.